BURN WHAT WILL BURN

ALSO BY CB McKENZIE

Bad Country

BURN WHAT WILL BURN

CB McKENZIE

Minotaur Books

A Thomas Dunne Book
New York

A THOMAS DUNNE BOOK FOR MINOTAUR BOOKS.
An imprint of St. Martin's Publishing Group.

BURN WHAT WILL BURN. Copyright © 2016 by CB McKenzie. All rights reserved. Printed in the United States of America. For information, address St. Martin's Press, 175 Fifth Avenue, New York, N.Y. 10010.

"Burn What Will Burn" (poem) copyright © 2016 by Alexander Long.

www.thomasdunnebooks.com
www.minotaurbooks.com

Library of Congress Cataloging-in-Publication Data

Names: McKenzie, C. B., author.
Title: Burn what will burn : a novel / C. B. McKenzie.
Description: First edition. | New York : Minotaur Books, 2016. | "A Thomas Dunne book."
Identifiers: LCCN 2016000052| ISBN 9781250083371 (hardcover) | ISBN 9781250083388 (ebook)
Subjects: LCSH: City and town life—Fiction. | BISAC: FICTION / Crime. | FICTION / Mystery & Detective / General. | GSAFD: Mystery fiction. | Suspense fiction.
Classification: LCC PS3613.C55566 B87 2016 | DDC 813/.6—dc23
LC record available at http://lccn.loc.gov/2016000052

Our books may be purchased in bulk for promotional, educational, or business use. Please contact your local bookseller or the Macmillan Corporate and Premium Sales Department at 1-800-221-7945, extension 5442, or by e-mail at MacmillanSpecial Markets@macmillan.com.

First Edition: June 2016

10 9 8 7 6 5 4 3 2 1

To
Mathew Madan
For
RoundTop

Every night I am in the same seared scene, a dream:
Where my dead tell me to burn what will burn,
Starting with them as a paperpoem ream.
—Alexander Long

BURN WHAT WILL BURN

CHAPTER 1

The body floated stubbornly in The Little Piney Creek, one and four tenths miles of graded dirt almost due south on Poe County Road 615 from my place, what used to be the Old Duncan Place.

I had stopped my morning constitutional on the rusted iron bridge when I heard a hawk's plaintive screech. A familiar red tail settled atop a loblolly like a drop of brown paint on the tip of a bristle brush and cocked an eye at the water below him. A fish rose against the creek's green face and snapped at a bug.

My eye followed this, natural, series of events—the hawk looking down for food, the fish rising up for food—until I saw the body floating like a boat that was swamped but wouldn't sink.

It was late August. Summer had been nothing but a long drought so the creek was running low and heated piss-warm in the shallows. But on occasion those days, there was the slightest chill in the morning air, a harbinger of autumn, that caused a mist to overlay the sides of The Little Piney, soft-edged strips of fog that moved as the water moved only slower, a ghost of the creek detached and hovering, too light to stay in the world, but too heavy yet to be gone.

Under this suspended shroud, on the north side of the creek, the body was lodged between a downed tree and the red clay bank, partially obscured by leaves, but un-mistakably a big man in a red shirt and blue jeans.

"Oh shit," I said when I saw him there.

Steered into the angle created by the shoreline and the fallen tree, the body was wreathed in leaves that flipped lightside to darkside in the pulse of eddied water. The skull bounced rhythmically between bark and bank. The dead man's back heaved like he was learning his first hard lesson of breathing water.

I threw up over the steel rail of the bridge. Curdled moonshine, two hundred proof, splashed on the water, whisked away.

My watch said it was six oh seven a.m.

About as good a time as any.

Around the foundation of the bridge, riprap reposed at a steep angle. I tugged the laces tighter on my pricey new walking shoes and started down, slipped on the loose, sharp shards of crushed granite and only barely regained my footing on a shoreline narrow and slick as a side of cheap bacon.

It was only five yards downstream from that spot to the dead man, but I dawdled. It would be misleading to say that I stopped to "pray" per se, and so imply the posses-sion of a spiritual faculty I do not, in fact, possess. But in my stop position it would be fair to say that I "waited with hope."

What I was hoping for, in this instance, was that I had only imagined the corpse floating in The Little Piney Creek, and that this corpse would turn out to be a mere invention of my irregular way of thinking.

Because this dead man was not a problem I wanted to claim as mine, was a problem that probably needed a god or some strong medication to obscure.

But as I reached over the downed tree and pushed a shaky hand against the dead man's shoulder, the rough bark of the white oak reminded me that this particular peculiar circumstance was real and not imagined.

A cottonmouth loosed itself from a tangle of downed tree limbs on the opposite side of the creek and began to slither across the surface of the creek in that menacing way that watersnakes have that defies gravity and logic and in that way terrifies sensible, Christian people in order to remind them of Edenic Reality.

I watched the snake cross the creek, his arrowhead swimming side to side, like a pocket watch swinging on a golden chain gone green, mesmerizing. The pollen was so thick on the creek's face that the serpent's trail was as visible as a deer track through the woods.

I reached back and grabbed up a handful of riprap stones to throw at the cottonmouth. I did not come close to hitting it, but did dissuade the snake downstream. He must have been over six feet long. The same length as the dead man in the river, more or less.

"This is some shit, isn't it?" I asked the dead man.

The dead man nodded, agreeing with me or with some conversational creature sunk in the mud a couple of feet below his face, his guide to the other side maybe.

I pushed him slightly.

The corpse was, I suppose, what is called a "floater" so he bobbed like a bottom-weighted buoy from the pressure I had applied to him. My stomach roiled and I swallowed some corn liquor bile, took ten deep breaths and "centered" myself (as some psychotherapist had once taught me to do in order to manage my anxiety). My anxiety, however, did not return to its normal, free-floating level, even after ten deep breaths.

I shoved him again, harder. He rolled onto a shoulder, but didn't show his face. I cracked back a few branches of the downed tree and touched a fingerend to the bruised depression at the base of his skull.

That bruise did not look good to me. In fact, it looked like a factor that would compound the problem.

I patted the back pockets of his blue jeans and found a couple of packaged condoms—XXL size—and a bullet about as long as my little finger. No gun nearby, though, not on the bank and not in the mud of the shallow water I filtered through my fingers.

I stuck the unfired cartridge in the pocket of my short pants along with the Trojans.

I searched all the pockets of the dead man, pants and shirt, and found he had no wallet on him, no car keys.

But looped on his leather belt was a large leather knife scabbard, empty but with the word, or name, "Buck" stamped on it. The scabbard looked big enough for Jim Bowie's knife.

"Buck" was a heavy bastard and, small as I am, it took all my strength to drag him out of the creek and when I had his body beached I was gasping at the air and my walking shoes and short pants were filthy with wet, red clay, my arms and hands covered to the elbows with mud and what I suppose was corpse slime.

The dead man's head rested between my knees, face in the red clay of the creekside. When I pushed him off, Buck fell on his back and his whole body seemed to exhale a malodorous fart.

I am not a doctor, a mortician or a policeman in any conventional understandings of those jobs. I was just a dyspeptic poet with a little family money. So I did not hazard a guess as to the cause or causes of the dead man's death. Though that big bruise on the back of his head did not, as said, look good.

Buck was hirsute with dark hair thick on his head where the flesh had not been nibbled away by fish or snapped away by turtles or pecked away by birds. Hair was thick even on his neck and arms.

There was a delicate gold wedding band depended on a thick gold link chain around Buck's neck. There was no inscription on the outside or inside of the ring, which was so thin there probably wasn't room for an inscription. The ring certainly could fit no finger of this big man, dead or alive.

I unclasped the chain and put it around my own neck, just for safekeeping.

Buck's eyelids were gone. Where his eyeballs had been were but black holes, though these spaces in his face seemed still, somehow, expressive; not so much expressing a particular emotion—of desire or loss, pain or joy—but as only empty vessels now waiting to be filled.

I swatted away the crawdads clinging to what was left of his lips and earlobes.

What remained of the dead man's nose was just a ridge of cartilage, dangled above vacant space by sinew, like a weird chicken bone suspended by fishing line over a garbage can.

Buck's exposed teeth were scary like a Halloween mask is scary—that is, so scary they did not even seem real.

I looked away from the dead man and leaned back. The sky had been made jigsaw by interlocking trees branches. I put a few blue pieces together then turned back to the dead man. He was still dead as a doorknob. And nobody to me, I decided. No one important to me at all.

———

I wanted to run away from the dead man in The Little Piney, but I'm not much of a runner. So I pulled him ashore and started another series of events, which is all history is really, mine and everybody's, just one damned thing after another.

I waited for a spell, waited for something/anything else to happen. I think I supposed someone, someone other than me and Buck, would appear. But the road I lived on was about as dead-ended as a road can be and still be a road. So . . .

No one appeared. Nothing helpful happened.

I'd spent much of the day before at my most local bar, in nearby Bertrandville. (There was no bar in Doker, my newish, nearest "hometown" of three hundred souls, and the whole county was dry but for the "members-only" establishments attached to hotels and country clubs, which were the only places for miles to buy a drink.) By early afternoon the day before I had been more than mildly drunk as is my regular wont.

So there were plenty of witnesses to my whereabouts that day before.

And during the early phase of my most recent bar-drunk, I had even written poems on paper napkins and distributed them liberally to my fellow patrons of the Crow's Nest Saloon and Grill. Then I watched the Cardinals play baseball on ESPN with the daily regulars, and then discussed mutual fund frontloading with the after-work crowd later on, and even later, slept away the early evening in my regular rented room at the Holiday Inn in which hostelry my Crow's Nest is housed and in which my domicile (Room 116, poolside) I pay for by the month because membership (that is, cash money) has its privileges.

The rest of the evening, after I fed my chickens and until dawn, was spent at home, returned inside my cups again watching videotapes of *Columbo* and *Rockford Files*.

Hence, the day before I'd have probably missed anybody driving down County Road 615 from ten a.m. on. Which meant that if my dead man in the creek, Buck, had come by my place the day before, I would not have seen hide nor hair of him.

So (I speculated, that is, hoped) my dead man in The Little Piney had passed by my deserted place, found the creek, fished awhile, imbibed a few cold ones maybe, tried to climb back up the steep slope of riprap, slipped as I had, fell, coshed himself on the back of his head, managed to return to the fallen oak tree, sat down for a rest, got woozy, blacked out, fell into the creek and drowned, in two feet of water as easy as in twenty. Buck had slipped, bumped his head and drowned. That seemed a satisfactory scenario. Happened all the time.

But where were his beer bottles? Where was his fishing tackle? His wallet and ID? His big hunting knife? The gun that went along with the bullet?

Most of all where was his vehicle?

"You shouldn't be out here," I told the corpse. How did you get *here* of all places?

Because I had never, in ten months and twenty-one days of local residence, seen a stranger at that spot on The Little Piney. That part of The Land o' Opportunity was just not someplace tourists wound up in, accidentally or on purpose. It was too far off Arkansas Scenic Highway 7 to attract visitors. The road was just brown dirt or red clay, gutted in places, ribbed in others. And it was no place in the world you could get to without a car or truck, a mule or a pair of willing feet in sensible walking shoes.

Only a few Locals ever went to that spot on The Little

Piney and only me and one other fella ever walked down here. Buck was not a Local that I knew of and he did not seem to me to be the type of fella to walk much of anywhere in his snakeskin cowboy boots. He also did not seem like a tourist—he seemed like a well-heeled hillbilly who would know his way around a creekside, drunk or not.

So it was hard to explain how, or why, Buck had gotten himself there dead in The Little Piney of all places.

I shrugged even though there was nobody to see me do it.

When you live a long time alone you just do things like that—shrug, nod, talk to yourself, or your chickens, the dead or God.

I have these habits of action, because, in general, I am as lonely as Adam before Eve appeared—living underneath a God who thinks of me as only a hobby of His, but in a Garden, more or less, of Plenty.

Thinking of Eden's Garden made me hungry for Miss Ollie's diner. I was missing my breakfast at EAT Cafe spending time with this dead Buck.

I tore a small branch off the water-soaked white oak, knelt beside the corpse, covered the dead man's face with the oak leaves, looked again at him.

On the inside of his right forearm was a crude tattoo of eagles rampant, the Stars and Stripes, the Marine Corps motto.

Semper Fidelis.

"If you say so, Buck," I suggested as an encomium.

I started up the bank.

Brush rustled under the trees on the opposite shore.

"Hello?" I called across the creek.

No answer.

I snatched a handful of riprap and threw the stones across the stream, almost.

"Hello!" I hailed a shadow.

I looked past the bridge toward a weedy twenty acres or so that was outlined by ten-foot-tall chain-link fencing decorated with loops of concertina wire and NO TRESPASSING and DANGER: NO OPEN BURNING signs.

A stone house was tucked in one corner of the untended spread. But no one lived there. Mine was the last inhabited place going in that direction for several miles past The Little Piney. Beyond which was nothing but a very bad, two-track road, deer trails and kudzu cloaked, dense-to-black forest, hardwood and softwood crowded thick and currently dried out as stacked, seasoned cordwood ready for a fire.

"Malcolm? Reverend Pickens? Isaac? Newton? Jacob?"

I named almost all the inhabitants of our isolated little hollow.

None of them answered me.

But someone was watching me.

This is not an unusual feeling for me to have. I have long lived with the ghosts of my departed and often sense my dead daddy, momma, my wife, our stillborn child hovering nearby me. At times I believe God is taking a too-keen interest in my simple affairs, intruding into my complicated thoughts like a bookmark stuck over and over again, willy-nilly in the pages of my life's odyssey, my crazy story.

But this was different because there was really someone there, on the other side of the creek, hiding in the bushes, watching me.

I didn't waste any more time trying to find out who, if anyone, was there spying on me from the other side of

The Little Piney. It was probably someone, or something I didn't want to know or even know about.

❧

Out of habit I stopped at my bullet-riddled mailbox. It was open, but empty, as per usual. The Star Route postman would not deliver rural mail to my rural house as he didn't approve of a Reynolds living at the Old Duncan Place since nobody but Duncans had ever lived there before me. Snow, rain, heat of day, gloom, etc., apparently did not dissuade local government employees of USPS from their appointed rounds, but delivering dividend statements to a nonLocal did.

The Locals had their own special reasoning about life and its operating procedures that I didn't even try to understand.

A black widow spider had constructed an elaborate web in the mailbox, which was but a metal box with a hinged lid on it, a lid that could be shut tight at any time. Still, she sat centered in her ignorance, waiting, doing her thing. If I closed the lid on the box, the spider would die. But I left the mailbox open because I admire patience and can appreciate making an innocent mistake as much as the next guy. Sometimes we set ourselves down in trouble through no fault of our own and only survive it because a god doesn't shut down the lid on our little box and cut off our life supplies.

I limped to the house to find my car keys so I could drive to a public telephone.

A blister bloomed on my left heel. I had paid a lot of money for my walking shoes, but they still did not fit me.

————

I don't have a phone for two reasons—either they ring or else they don't ring. They're bothersome to me either way, so I don't have one. Except for a couple of distant relations who are waiting impatiently for me to die, my neighborhood friend Malcolm and my stockbrokers and money managers in Fargo and Houston and elsewhere, nobody cares in the least where I'm at or what I'm doing there.

Most people need a phone, for emergencies if nothing else. But I didn't have any emergencies left in my life.

I didn't think of my discovery of the corpse in the creek as being any kind of emergency situation—not for me, at least. And Buck's emergency had passed. He was passed. In an hour he would be just as dead as he would be in another day or next week, forever dead, suffering or celebrating beyond this pale.

And the dead don't need me. Maybe sometimes they bother me, but never do they need me.

And I cling to the misguided belief that the dead, in general, somehow, consciously or subconsciously or unconsciously, bring their ends on themselves, by deed or else by nature.

So to protect my own self from death, purposeful or accidental, I don't keep straight razors or abusable pills or loaded weapons in the house and before I start any vocational drinking I hide my car keys from myself, because, sometimes, we can be our own worst and most dangerous enemies.

It took over nine minutes but I found the keys in the bathroom.

I slipped on dishwasher's gloves and extracted the key ring from the tank of the toilet, washed the keys in shampoo, rinsed them and dried them and sprayed them with disinfecting spray, ungloved and scrubbed my hands thoroughly with lye soap, cleaned out my fingernails with a stiff brush, smelled them.

They smelled faintly of corpse slime, so I redid the whole handwashing operation and topped it off with a rubbing alcohol rinse and a splash of bleach, dried off with toilet paper and flushed the paper down and out into the septic tank in the backyard.

I took a long but tepid shower, abusing my skin with the coarsest loofah available on the common market, then dried off with the coarsest bath towel available on the common market. I brushed my teeth until my gums bled, swallowed the toothpaste spit, then rinsed with Listerine for the prescribed two minutes, then scrubbed my face, again, with a wet sponge, put rubbing alcohol in my ears and nostrils and put a moleskin patch on my newest blister. I slathered my whole body in sunscreen, adding an extra dab to my bald spot, then proceeded to the bedroom and changed my dirty short pants for a clean pair of chinos, a fresh-from-the-package, white pocket T-shirt, antifungal cotton socks and another pair of expensive walking shoes that had been guaranteed to work cooperatively and efficaciously with my small and preposterously flat feet.

I wasn't hopeful.

⁂

By six forty-nine a.m. I was returned to the bathroom and examining my face, hairline, and waistline in the crooked mirror hanging above the sink.

I looked the same as per usual.

I did feel a slight twinge of nausea, but I have felt a slight twinge of nausea every day of my life.

If anybody had been there to ask me, I would have said, automatically, that I was fine.

CHAPTER 2

Poe County Road 615 is an antique farm-to-market thoroughfare that resembles one rumpled leg of a pair of washed-out corduroy trousers. I steered my battered old pickup in the smoother wales. Behind me exhaust thick enough to slice poured out of a clanging tailpipe.

Three-tenths of a mile east of my place was the First Rushing Evangelical True Bible Prophecy Church of the Rising Star in Jesus Christ.

WELCOME ALL, a large but rusty metal sign planted in the hardpack dirt parking lot greeted the Faithful and the Prospective. WELCOME ALL, SERVICES AT 8:30 AM SUNDAY, THE LORD'S DAY, the sign informed. THE CORRECT AND GOOD NEWS AS PROCLAIMED BY THE GOSPEL AND DELIVERED BY THE RIGHT REVEREND JOE PICKENS, SENIOR, MINISTER OF THE FAITH, it promised.

This sign seemed a bit redundant on several counts, but it worked somewhat for Mean Joe. Even though the Preacher Pickens was acknowledged, hands down, as being the most mean man in Rushing and surrounding areas all the way into Oklahoma on the one side and Missouri on the other side, and was suspected of being even one of the meanest men in the whole of the Ozarks, and even though he preached every week in one of the most isolated hollows in all of the Americas, the hallowed grounds of the Right Reverend Joe Pickens, Senior, still hosted at least ten vehicles a week, which might not seem like a lot, but it was. A hundred and twenty-two yards farther "down the hill"—as was said locally to establish latitude and longitude (meaning south, toward the river)— was the Wellses' spread, a double-wide mobile home that could never be moved because of all the trash piled around it like an Osage Indian village barricade and because of all the anchored additions attached to it—decks and patios and garages and carports and storage sheds and two aboveground swimming pools (the one simply abandoned when the algae in it solidified to the point where seedlings started taking root and the swimming pool became a sort of virgin island)—and giant dog houses for their giant dogs—rottweilers on the east end of the house with Great Danes on the west end and two types of pit bulls, one penned on the north side of the trailer house the other on the south side. . . .

This whole extravagance of rural riches, this decomposing and ever-expanding fiefdom of valued trash, was set up on a knoll denuded by chicken-scratching and dog-digging and kid-playing and was boundaried by almost a half mile of pooched-out chain-link fencing and surrounded by acres of the most comprehensive collection of white trash necessities imaginable, including a finite but uncountable number of jacked-up and rusted-out car and truck and SUV and tractor and school bus and ambulance and hearse and ATV and motorcycle chassis (many of them so kudzu-covered they seemed organic), as well as an armada of holey boats (from Sunfishes to Glastron trihulls, to oceangoing whalers to a dozen johnboats, scuttled Skeeters, even a real birch-bark canoe gone to rot with a river willow growing out of it), enough wood pallets to set that part of the world on fire, every playground set available at Walmart and even a life-size plywood nativity scene established year round in the front yard, this assembly of the Holy so shrouded in red clay dust all the Wise Men looked like the Cleveland Indian.

A pair of very small bore rifle barrels rested on the shoulders of a brace of these headless Wise (Red) Men.

One of the little Wells bastards shot at me.

Another star materialized on my windshield.

I leaned on the truck's horn.

It wheezed asthmatically.

"Reynolds Queerbait!" one of the twins yelled.

Jacob and Faith Sue Wells and their diabolical set of eight-year-olds, Isaac and Newton, had a telephone, but I never asked to use it.

For obvious reasons.

Another BB pellet, losing steam, clattered into the bed of my pickup.

Neighbors.

℃◍

Two point six miles of uninhabited country later the truck stalled as I steered off County Road 615 near the intersection of that dirt road and the pavement of a semi-major state road. I coasted past the gas pumps of Pick's General Store and UPUMPIT! and handbraked beside the mud-encrusted, freestanding phone booth.

When I unhooked the bailing wire from the glove box, pickup paraphernalia exploded onto the floorboard like Fibber McGee's closet junk. I tucked my big fat wallet back in the box but held on to a prescription bottle of the tiny tranquilizers my physician, Dr. Doc Williams, allowed me.

Atarax, they are called, a pharmaceutical advertising word derived from the Greek *ataraxia*, which means "a state of robust calm," which was a state I liked to dwell in, far from the state of distress; but it was hit or miss with me, from day to day, where I landed, with medication or without it.

I could, as medically advised, take six pills a day. I wanted twenty. There were only three left. I showed restraint and took two.

I dialed 911 even though I was in no emergency, just to take advantage of what my local tax dollars paid for.

The phone went, bzzz clickety click. Then nothing for a long time.

I hung up.

Taxes.

In the skinny directory for Doker, Arkansas, a little town just less than three miles east of UPUMPIT!, on Scenic Highway 7, more or less, I found the number for police, rummaged in my pocket for change, found a solitary quarter, slotted it, and called the nearest constabulary, which was manned, as far as I knew, by only one constable, an octogenarian who had not appeared outside his house for over a year.

The phone of the Doker Constable rang twenty-one times before I hung up.

Cops.

The phone ate my two bits.

I tried 911 again.

Just clickety click bzzz this time, or rather, nothing useful again.

Telephones.

The screen door to Pick's General Store and UPUMPIT! banged open and the proprietor's teenaged grandson, Malcolm Ray Pickens, yelled my name, more or less.

"Bob Reynold!"

Malcolm was even more undersized and anemic than me and some shy of a full load, but about the best adjusted person I had ever known, which said more about my dead family and lost friends than it did about Malcolm, I would hazard.

He leaned into the booth, seemed glad to see me. I wished I was in a better mood for him.

There was a bruise on his forehead, purple and uneven as a Concord grape smashed and rolled flat into raw bread dough.

When I tried to touch it he jerked his head away and then fingered lank hair over the injury.

"Your PaPaw been hitting you again, Malcolm?"

The kid shook his head, then shrugged, then nodded since the kid seemed congenitally unable to lie.

"Loan me some money for a phone call, Malcolm Ray."

"You good for it, Bob Reynold?"

All I had to do was frown.

I gave Malcolm ten bucks a week just to feed the chickens on my front porch, which, apart from his snakeskin wallet–selling business, was all the money he ever got from the world.

He pulled a fistful of small change out of his overalls and handed it over.

"Just playing with you, Bob Reynold."

"I'm not in a playful mood," I said, which was not news.

I thumbed quarters into the phone box, hesitated, considered forgetting about it, the corpse, the dead man, Buck. But it seemed too late for that to happen. Wheels within wheels, cogs, that is, were turning and I was stuck up their works it seemed like, whether I liked that position or not.

"What you thinking on, Bob Reynold?"

Malcolm stood outside and pressed his nose against the dirty phone booth, smearing his sweet face into a malevolent mask.

I slapped the glass. Malcolm backed against the truck, hitched up his overalls.

"I's just asking, Bob Reynold."

"I'm trying to think," I said, with more heat than I had intended, I guess, because Malcolm's face drooped.

"I'm sorry, Malcolm."

The kid nodded to accept my apology.

"I can see you upset, Bob Reynold. So I figure it's something eating at you. I can sure tell when it is and it especial is right about now."

"You're a genius, Malcolm."

The kid snuffed.

"I appreciate your concern, Malcolm Ray," I corrected myself, sincerely enough.

Nobody else gave much of a thought to my condition save for Malcolm, so I needed to be grateful for that, difficult as his concern was to deal with sometimes.

"You know what PaPaw say about it, Bob Reynold—it's dangerous to think too much on a thing like you do, because all you own thinking it crowd out the message of the Lord. Thinking too much make you bad crazy, Bob Reynold. That's what's got my own daddy in such the state he be in—listening to his ownself and not to the Lord God. Turned my daddy into a dangerous elephant in this here communerty, what it did."

"Dangerous element" was clear enough, but I didn't know what "community" Malcolm was referring to. What had once been the regular little town of Rushing, Arkansas, seemed to me to be reduced to Malcolm Ray and Mean Joe, Jacob, Faith Sue and their twins, and me and my chickens.

Joe Pickens Junior, Malcolm's daddy, a notorious, but small-time drug dealer, had not been around Rushing for years. The kid's mother was, reportedly, a dog track whore in West Memphis. His grandfather, Joe Pickens Senior,

Mean Joe, the Right Reverend Pickens, had raised Malcolm insofar as Malcolm had been raised. It was speculated locally that the rest of Malcolm's family—grandparents, cousins, etc.—all no-goods by standard measures and with varying criminal degrees, had been disappeared by the Right Reverend Mean Joe Pickens Senior himself or by God Himself.

"Steada selling them drugs and beating the bushes like he been done, my daddy'd been better off turning it all over to the Lord Jehovah God, Bob Reynold. Putting it in the hands of Jesus Rising Star, like I do."

That faith was all well and good for Malcolm, but did not help me much then or ever.

I waited ten seconds for a sign from God anyway—this stupid habit my momma had cursed me with, she being one of those gut-wrenching born-agains who seemed always on the point of absolute Despair or else absolute Rapture and never on any level ground, spiritual, intellectual, psychological or emotional.

But I loved her.

I guess I did.

She had been dead fifteen years December twenty-first next and

Heaven still, was empty,

Of signs, of clouds,

As Per Usual.

❧

I dialed my favorite bartender.

"Crow's Nest. Smarty Bell, Proprietor, speaking."

The Crow's Nest was the saloon in the Holiday Inn and Convention Center of Bertrandville, Arkansas, a small city eight point six miles north of Doker, my "hometown," on Scenic Highway 7. Smarty Bell was head bartender and part-owner of the Nest, so he was there almost eighteen hours a day except for Sundays, when the Nest was forcibly closed by local ordinances and on Mondays when he was sleeping off Sundays. Or else was fishing for (only trophy-size, as he said) bigmouth bass in his rigged-out, high-gloss, high-octane-powered Skeeter boat. Or chasing after his girlfriend, a stripper who was even glossier, more high-octane and more high-maintenance than his fishing rig.

The constable was not answering his phone, 911 was on the fritz and my lawyers were in states other than Arkansas, so since Smarty Bell was as close as I had to a sensible acquaintance he got the call.

I pressed the receiver against my shoulder. "Could you go get my mail for me, Malcolm Ray?"

The kid nodded, lounged off toward the store.

"Hello," I said into the phone. "It's Bob."

"It's a little early for a liquor call, Buddy. Even for you. Need some 'shine to go?"

"No," I said, rubbing my temples. "I surely do not."

I had dispensed with a quart Mason jar the night before and would have been unable to hit a barn door with a thrown handful of dry beans from a foot distance most of the evening.

"You're going to kill yourself, Buddy."

I had been warned about that before and that had not happened yet, for whatever reasons there were.

It's hard to kill cockroaches too.

"I need some advice, Smarty Bell."

"Still got Tammy Fay Trouble, Bud?"

"No," I lied. "I'm over that."

Since I had first seen the young woman, almost ten months before, I had been seriously smitten by Tammy

Fay Smith, hung around her place whenever she'd allow it, paid for unneeded and inexpert repairs on the old Ford truck she had oversold me for twice Blue Book value.

Tammy Fay was just the kind of woman you'd pay to watch sweat.

She had let me kiss her once, seven and a half months before, and that encounter in her garage had had all the trappings of a failed experiment, major head-butting and misplaced lips because of my diminutiveness. She shrugged me off like a fly when it was done and had not gotten as close as ten feet to me since, but not a day went by I didn't recall the incident.

Some women just make you forget what a smart fellow you are.

The mechanic girl had told me in no uncertain terms that I was not her type and never would be, even if my investment portfolio trebled, even if I got hair implants, even if I pledged my life to her.

Women.

But I could see the woman's point—which point poked both ways: If someone was someone I wanted then they were my type and me not being their type did not alter them being my type and what I wanted.

"What would you do if you found a body in The Little Piney?" I asked the bartender.

A vacuum cleaner whirred in the Crow's Nest in Bertrandville, a bar rag squeaked in a glass. My watch set the time at seven twenty-eight in the a.m. The world was waked up and tending to business as per usual. The quick of the world, at least, were tending to business. The dead? I didn't know what they were tending to, but maybe they were tending to their business too.

"Say again, Buddy."

"It's a man," I provided as a start. "Big fellow."

"Colored or white?"

"Kind of grayish." I described the waterlogged corpse.

"Say what?"

"Caucasian."

"How old?"

"Late thirties, early forties maybe. But I'm just guessing. Why? You know him based on that?"

"I heard Joe Pickens Junior jumped bail over in West Memphis last week. You know who I'm talking about?"

"Mean Joe's son, the dope dealer," I said. "Malcolm's daddy."

"Retard's daddy, right," Smarty Bell said. "Friend of mine from college, Ricky Dale Hart, works for local law enforcement sometimes and he advised me I should keep an ear out, because it's a reward for information about Joe Junior."

"Why? Is Joe Pickens Junior some kind of big fish?"

"Nope. But Poe County Sheriff wants Joe Junior bad and so there's bounty hunters after him too."

"What did Malcolm's daddy do this time?" I asked.

"Joe Junior used to run a lot of very primo Arkansaweed, hereabouts and aroundabouts, and even pimped a bit over in Danielles."

"Did Joe Pickens Junior get busted?"

"Joe Junior's gotten busted here and there and everywhere," said Smarty Bell. "But mostly for minor possession raps or drunk and disorderlies that did not amount to minnow shit. But then Joe Junior got busted in West Memphis for possession with intent to distribute to minors, and on middle school property, what I heard from Ricky Dale. Being a multiple offender, and actually peddling on school property, Joe Junior's in a deep shithole now without a shovel or a rope. Then he jumped bail. And that's not the first time that's happened."

"That all sounds bad for Joe Pickens Junior," I said, thinking about the son of Joe Pickens Junior, Malcolm, who had enough on this plate to worry about without having his daddy on the lam. "Do you think Joe Junior is hereabouts?" I asked.

"He might be around, because dumb crooks always go home and Joe Junior is one dumb crook."

"What will happen to Joe Junior if he gets caught?" I asked.

"Him getting caught is not the problem for him," Smarty Bell said, elliptically, I thought.

"What does that mean, Smarty Bell?"

"It means Joe Junior might be bathing with the big-mouth bass if Sheriff Baxter is aimed at him. Baxter hates Joe Pickens Junior."

"Why?"

"Could not say in particular," said Smarty Bell. "I think Joe Junior looked at the sheriff wrong one day or threw up on him during a D&D arrest and that was that. Sam Baxter is one of those black and white guys. If Sam Baxter is 'for' you, then you are golden. But if Sam Baxter's 'against' you, you best just go away from this country and leave no forwarding address."

I preferred not to deal with Manicheans myself, but the world was full of people who saw no shades of gray, not even on cloudy days.

"So you think this man I found is Joe Pickens Junior? He had a Semper Fi tattoo," I said. "Real big fellow. Red cowboy shirt."

"Not striking a chord," Smarty Bell said. "Not Joe Junior, for sure. Wrong type. Joe Junior was never in any armed services and he's skinny as a rail. Maybe this dead fella was a fisherman?"

"Nobody fishes at that spot on The Little Piney but me and Malcolm and the Wells twins. Everybody else goes over the state park if they're fishing The Little Piney."

It was too hard to get to the water at that location on the little creek and with no place to park and not much bank to sit on, too many snakes and turtles, not enough fish, it was definitely only a Local's spot an outsider wouldn't stumble on or stay in, a fishing hole without any advertisable attractions, where you went only if you didn't have anyplace else to go or because it was your own backyard. Not the kind of place you wound up in by accident.

"No ID on him?" Smarty Bell asked me.

"Nothing."

I touched the gold ring that was under my shirt, depended by the gold chain around my neck.

"No car keys? Car?"

"Nope."

"He was dumped then," Smarty Bell said surely. "Somebody killed him elsewhere, drove to the bridge and tossed him in."

"Is that a regular thing around here?"

"It's happened before. Not there exactly, but nearby there. In South Slough. Couple of years ago they drug out a tourist lady who'd been raped and then beat to death and left in the mud to drown. They had some suspicions about who done it, but never could make a case against anybody."

"I was thinking my situation could have been an accident. Maybe the fella I found just slipped and hit his head, then fell in the creek and drowned."

I was hoping someone could conceivably think this actually.

The bartender grunted, said nothing for a moment.

"Autopsy'll tell," said Smarty Bell. He paused. I waited

because I did not have much else to do. "But your fella, he didn't walk to The Little Piney. No regular people walk down there."

"I do," I reminded.

"You're not an example of anything regular, Buddy," Smarty Bell reminded.

That was the sticker in explaining how the dead man had gotten to The Little Piney. Nobody walked anywhere anymore, but me, it seemed, and Malcolm. Even the twins rode their motorized three-wheeler to the creek when they went down there to blow up frogs with firecrackers or skin live snakes, animal torture being one of their primary hobbies.

The dead man had not walked to The Little Piney. No way. Nobody would believe that. But if he hadn't walked, where was his vehicle?

"What should I do, Smarty Bell?" I asked. "911 was a wash. I tried the Doker Constable and he didn't answer."

"I think the Doker Constable's been dead for about six months, just nobody's saying anything so his widow woman can keep collecting his checks. And the B'ville cops probably are all out sick from regular duty since there's a strike going on at the Tidy Chicken plant over in Danielles by the Marshall Islanders, so I imagine the local cops and deputies are all over there across the river at Danielles pulling security shifts for extra cash. The cops around here make more money working for the chicken plant than they do working for City and County."

"Should I call State Police?"

Smarty Bell did not answer me immediately. I waited.

"Call Sam Baxter," he advised, as if some thought had gone into that suggestion. "That's his bailiwick and he'll be pissed royal if he's called off the bench last minute."

"Baxter's the sheriff of Poe County?" I asked, thinking he sounded familiar.

"*High* Sheriff of Poe County. And yeah, you know him," said Smarty Bell, as if he knew him and did not like him and expected me to feel likewise. "He's in here all the time. Trolling. And he knows you, Buddy. Asking after you just the other day. Wanted to know what I knew about you and Miss Tammy Fay."

"What did you tell him about me and her?"

"I told him I know about you and her, what the Pope knows about tampons."

I didn't say anything for a moment.

"Is the sheriff after Tammy Fay?"

"Baxter's after pretty much everybody," Smarty Bell said.

Malcolm came out of the store with one of his pet rat snakes wrapped around his forearm and no mail. He snapped his fingers and returned inside, came back with a clutch of envelopes and a couple of magazines.

"I'll call the sheriff," I said.

"Might as well, Buddy. My guess is, Baxter'll jump in on it anyway. That's his neck of the woods from way back. Look better if you call him first."

"I want to do the right thing."

"Suit yourself on that, Buddy. Just remember you didn't talk to me," Smarty Bell said. "Because me and Baxter do not make music. He tried to bust my ass for some bullshit once and I hadn't forgot about that yet. I'm just as black and white as that asshole is when it comes to grudges."

Malcolm strolled to the perpetually lowered tailgate of my truck and draped his snake over the sidewall of the bed, started examining my mail. The snake slid into the shade under the pickup.

"And when you get in touch with him, do not be no smart-ass either, Buddy. Baxter is always loaded for bear. Do not give him any shit."

"Why would I?"

"Who knows why you would? You just got a habit of crawling under people's skin. Sometimes you put folks off. You're not exactly socialized, Buddy. You talk funny and write poems. Regulars here think you're a half-cocked loose cannon, you want to know."

"All right," I mumbled.

I thought the boozehounds at the Crow's Nest liked me.

They just liked my free financial advice I guess.

"Not me thinks you're wacked, Buddy. I like weirdos and you tip, so I think you're okay. I'm just saying, don't be exactly your regular self around High Sheriff Baxter," the bartender warned. "It's generally rumored he takes rides in the country with people he doesn't like and comes back with an empty shotgun seat. Probably not true, but could be, if you hear me. One word to the wise should be sufficient, Buddy."

"I appreciate you, Smarty Bell."

"All right then," Smarty Bell said. "See you around the well, Buddy."

Smarty Bell hung up.

I hung up.

The pay phone kicked out the change, which made sense because it was Malcolm's money not mine.

I located a number under "Poe County Emergency Services" and dialed that number in Bertrandville.

"Poe County Sheriff's Department," a woman twanged.

She sounded just like Tammy Wynette.

"I'd like to speak with Sheriff Baxter, please."

"The sherf's out of touch at the present moment."

"How about a deputy then?"

"Depties are pretty much all at the Tidy Chicken plant in Danielles."

"It's an emergency," I lied.

"For emergencies please dial the number nine, then the number one and then the number one again, please."

"I know what 911 is. I tried 911."

"Well?"

"Well, it didn't work," I said.

"It's got to work, Sir," the dispatcher insisted. "It's 911."

"Well, it does not work from where I'm at."

"Please don't use that tone of voice with me, please, Sir. Wait, please."

It was getting very hot in the phone booth.

"Try again, please," the dispatcher instructed.

She hung up.

"Shit."

"You okay, Bob Reynold?" Malcolm called to me.

"Fine as the hair on a frog," I grumbled.

I counted to ten and back to zero, took a deep breath, tried 911 again.

Bzzz, click, clickety click, bzzz, nothing.

Forgetting about the corpse was seeming a better option as the minutes passed. Was it too late to return to The Little Piney and push him back into the water? The local aquatic fauna would probably have him disposed of relatively quickly as a full-grown snapping turtle could bite a man's leg off given enough time.

But now Smarty Bell knew about the corpse in the creek.

"Who you trying to call, Bob Reynold?"

"The sheriff," I said.

Malcolm scratched in his greasy hair, looked at me sideways.

"Why is that, Bob Reynold?"

"Bob Reynolds's business," I told him.

Malcolm frowned, shrugged.

"He in town this morning," Malcolm said, reluctantly it seemed. "I overseen him eating in the café around about six."

I knew Sam Baxter's face from newspaper dots in the local rag, and had seen Sam Baxter around and about in Bertrandville (sometimes especially at the Crow's Nest, as Smarty Bell had reminded me); but I had never seen Sam Baxter in Doker. And I was in Doker almost every day for something, had a running tab at and seldom missed breakfast at EAT. Most usual mornings I would get to town even before Miss Ollie Ames opened the café and sit my truck on Elm Street for reasons of my own.

I slotted coin, dialed a Doker number.

"This is EAT. Miss Ollie Ames speaking."

"This is Bob Reynolds, Miss Ollie. I'm looking for the sheriff, Sam Baxter. Would you know if he's around?"

"He was for a fact," the owner of the café informed me. "Earlier. But he's gone now. Hang on, Mister Reynolds . . ."

I hung on, stared at my watch. The second hand was not moving. It was seven thirty-three. I tapped the plastic crystal and the sweep hand moved three seconds and stopped again.

"My son says sheriff's still across the street at the Old Lion, Mister Reynolds."

The Old Lion had been a gas station and so that was what Locals persisted in calling Tammy's Tune-ups and Towing Service.

"At Tammy Fay's," I repeated.

"My son says, he's been over there at the garage awhile."

Her son, Warnell Ames, a hulking halfwit, should know—all he did, all day long, was sit on a stool out front of his momma's restaurant and stare at the Old Lion, hoping to catch a glimpse of Tammy Fay and watch the cars go by, lifting a hand in greeting to every single one.

I suppose that was a life of a sort though, like the rest.

"All right," I said. "Thank you, Miss Ollie."

"You got some troubles out your way, Mister Reynolds?"

"A small trouble."

"You're all right, though? Nothing happened to you, did it, Mr. Reynolds?"

"I'm fine," I said, kneading my eyeballs with my knuckles.

"I'm just thinking of you, Mister Reynolds."

"Thank you, Miss Ollie."

"Well, I worry about you, Mister Reynolds. Living way out there all alone. I've missed you at breakfast these last few days."

"I'm afraid I've been sick, Miss Ollie."

"I pray it was nothing serious, Mister Reynolds."

"It was nothing serious, Miss Ollie."

"You want me to holler over at the sheriff for you, Mister Reynolds?"

"I'll call the Old Lion myself. I've got the number."

Tammy Fay seldom opened her place before ten, if she opened it at all. She was never showered and dressed before nine. So the sheriff had most likely disturbed her at her apartment over the garage.

"My son thinks the sheriff's looking for somebody, Mister Reynolds."

"Well, Miss Ollie," I said. "Maybe I found somebody."

CHAPTER 3

"You get him, Bob Reynold?"

I nodded at Malcolm, thumbed in another quarter and dialed a memorized number in Doker. My stomach clenched listening to the phone in the Old Lion ring. Tammy Fay picked up on the fifth trill, clearing her throat.

"Yeah?"

She sounded as good as Bette Davis on a bad day.

"Tammy? It's me," I said. "Bob."

I could smell her honey-colored, smoky hair through the telephone line.

I felt a bit nauseated.

Tammy Fay coughed.

"You need to quit smoking," I said.

"There's a health warning printed right on the side of my Pall Malls, so I don't really need to hear this shit from you, do I? I have a doctor, you know. And you ain't him."

She was obviously in a foul mood, a place she could get to early and stay until late.

"I'm just looking for the sheriff," I said meekly.

"So?"

"I heard he was there."

"What do you need him for?"

"Business, I guess. Is he there?"

"He's just leaving."

"Stop him. Please."

"What for?"

She sounded really pissed.

"Forget it," I said. "I don't want to trouble you. I'll just call the dispatcher."

"Jesus," she said, coughed.

A car horn honked, echoed loud in the garage of the Old Lion. It sounded like the phone got dropped on the Doker end. Tammy Fay's guard dog, Stank, a near hairless, three-legged, bluetick hound bitch set up a racket of growling and barking.

A man's voice, raised above the racket, said, "Change your, something, mind. Something, something, straighten something out. You better, girl, something, think. If you had something to do . . ."

A car door slammed.

Tammy Fay, her voice pitched hoarse near a scream and far away from the telephone, yelled, "Fuck something, something. He something, something. I will leave, something, goddamn you and the rest of them, something, something. Fuck him. Fuck you. Fuck alla you!"

Or words to that sketchy effect.

Then clearly,

"I don't know what he wanted."

I waited for the Old Lion telephone to get recradled.

I was surprised to hear the distinctive clink of a Zippo cigarette lighter unhinging. Stank's barking was persistent still, but muffled, as if she had been locked in the back room.

"Hello," I said.

There sounded from the Old Lion in Doker a heavy exhalation, a smoker blowing smoke.

"Tammy Fay?"

"Who's calling?" a man asked.

I didn't answer.

I waited.

Whoever was on the other end of the line waited too, outwaited me.

"This is Bob Reynolds," I admitted.

"Randy Reynolds, the fellow that bought the Old Duncan Place," I was immediately placed, but misnamed.

"Bob Reynolds," I corrected. "Is this Sheriff Baxter?"

"Randall Robert Reynolds," he said, like he was testing my names for flaws.

"Star Route 1, Box 98M," I added my address, just so he would be sure who I was.

"I know where you live, Mr. Reynolds," he said.

"Are you Sheriff Sam Baxter?"

He cleared his throat, said, "You got business with me, Mr. Reynolds," which sounded, as delivered, more a statement of fact than a question.

"Yes," I said, leaned against the wall of the phone booth, wiped the sweat off my face with a sleeve of my T-shirt. "I found a body."

He cleared his throat. "I asked a question."

"Did you hear me?"

"Yes, Mr. Reynolds," he answered. "I hear you. You claim to have found a dead man."

"Yes."

It was a man.

"You're at Pick's place," he said.

"Yes. At UPUMPIT!"

That, I supposed, was a natural assumption, if he knew where I lived and knew that I didn't have a telephone. That seemed quite a bit to know, though, about a total stranger.

How natural the assumption was that the corpse was a man, I didn't know. Seemed that was a fifty-fifty shot without insider knowledge.

"Stay where you're at then, Mr. Reynolds," he instructed. "I'll be out shortly."

He hung up.

The receiver slipped out of my slick grip, banged against the phone booth wall. I wiped my palms dry on my new T-shirt, replaced the receiver.

Malcolm was staring at me.

"You all right, Bob Reynold?"

My skin was clammy and the narrow band that is always around my chest constricted. I took in and let out ten deep breaths, escaped the stifling heat of the phone booth, leaned into the cab of the truck, fetched my bottle of tranquilizers, tipped the final pill into my mouth, swallowed it with cotton-dry spit.

I walked around the parking lot of Pick's, counted from zero to one hundred and back to zero. I had hoped the day would be over quick, but it now augured the opposite, and appeared to be one of those stretched-out days that take as long to get rid of as a hangover.

"I say, you all right, Bob Reynold?"

Malcolm was shadowing me as I paced.

"Go get us a couple of Coca-Colas," I suggested. "Tell your PaPaw I'll be in shortly to sign the chit."

Malcolm shuffled to the store and banged through the screen door. I sat down on the tailgate of the truck, tucked up my legs for fear of the snake resting under the pickup.

Some of my mail was opened, but I didn't mind. Malcolm could hardly read a stop sign, but the kid liked to look over my bank statements and quarterly reports, pretend he was a businessman. I never got anything more personal than those or *Poetry Magazine* and *Investor's Weekly* anyway.

To distract myself I skimmed an account summary from First National Bank of Bertrandville which told me how much I was worth in Arkansas, then scanned a few other missives of a fiduciary type to refresh my memory about how much I was worth in North Dakota, New York, Texas and elsewhere.

"That banking stuff, Bob Reynold?"

I nodded.

I've never been entirely comfortable with my money. It has never seemed my own, but always my daddy's who was a sort of stock character, the Midwestern Business-man who goes somewhat global, but whose wife stayed at home and still shopped at the Salvation Army and spent most of her time at church.

I would complain about my daddy, but he did always maintain me, if not in high style at least in some style. He really, simply ignored me. And his success in the world did not ever really rub off on me, but not a lot does rub off on me—my skin is as thick against success as it is against failure.

Malcolm handed me a bottle of Coca-Cola. Ice oozed up the curved neck. I sucked out the frozen soda pop.

The kid hung on the sidewall of the pickup, resting on his armpits, slack as a heat-struck snake. True South, Mal-colm was a boy who knew a hundred ways to take a load off and save his strength in deadening heat.

"You rich as Solomon's mind, ain't you, Bob Reynold?"

"Near enough to suit me," I admitted.

Malcolm nodded like that was important information.

"And where you get it all from again?"

The kid had trouble understanding that most of the rich people in the world didn't earn their wealth with good ideas and hard work.

I'd never had a real career. Just hung around and pre-tended to be a poet until money came to me and then in-vested it, prudently. I am a cautious but shrewd investor with pathologically plain tastes who can be very aggres-sive when the mood strikes but seldom makes a move in the market or elsewhere without assaying the risks and covering my ass.

My stockbroker says I am an opportunistic predator. Camouflaged.

"Inheritance," I reminded the kid. "My parents died. And then my wife . . ."

"She drug overdose because y'all's baby pass," the kid reminded me.

I had told him about my wife, how I'd met her during graduate school where we were both "poets" of some but not the same sort—as I could actually write a bit and she could only pose as a poet—then courted her, bought her a (nice and classic, I thought) used Cadillac, married her, indulged and endured her alive, suffered her dead, insured her to the hilt.

Malcolm figured my wife and I had needed Jesus in our life to make our marriage work. Which was exactly what he thought everybody needed about everything. If you didn't catch fish you needed Jesus. If you had a headache or got a rash or fell down the steps you needed Jesus. If you lost your car keys you needed Jesus, etc., etc.

I, actually, could not argue with him about all that. Because who knew why you lost your car keys when you knew right where you had put them, why your mother got lung cancer when neither she nor anybody around her ever smoked, why some watermelons would be just the right firm and sweet and some mealy and soured and inedible and all from the same patch, planted and picked on the same days?

"Your explanation is close enough to the truth to be its cousin," I told my friend.

Malcolm did not seem to be pondering out my statement. He looked at me and squinted.

"My daddy sell dope. You think he kill you wife wit his dope?"

"No, Malcolm." I shook my head. "Your daddy selling Arkansaweed had nothing to do with my wife's death way down in Texas."

"You sure, Bob Reynold? You know my daddy he very successful at dope selling. And they say his dope is pretty strong."

"I'm fairly certain your daddy did not have anything to do with my wife's death, Malcolm." Indeed, I knew for a fact it didn't.

"You swear on Jesus Rising Star?"

"Sure," I said because it never bothered me to swear to any useful statements. "I swear on Jesus Rising Star."

Malcolm was quiet for a long moment. I imagined he was reflecting on Death and the Hereafter or some other religious topic. But he was not.

"I don't 'spect I'll get anything when he pass, will I?"

"Who you mean, Malcolm?" I asked.

"Daddy," he said. "And PaPaw. Momma if she aroun'. I won't get no 'heritance from any them, will I?"

I shook my head, because it didn't seem at all likely Malcolm would inherit anything from his people. Most weed dealers in that area, once everything was said and done, netted less money than the waitresses at Shoney's, all lived like trash and absolutely always wound up nailed and jailed. And Mean Joe's place of business, UPUMPIT!, and his church were mortgaged to the hilt, from what Miss Ollie Ames at EAT had told me, so Malcolm wouldn't get anything when his granddad Pickens died either, save for crippling debt or, if he was lucky, a big fat zero and some help from Social Services.

I stared at my financial statements. I had nearly enough

money to burn a wet mule, but you usually can't buy what you want.

Maybe that's why I lived like I did, like I didn't have anything. Because I couldn't have what I wanted anyway. Maybe I was just genetically cheap. That accusation had been made.

"So what were you doing downtown, Malcolm Ray?" I flipped our conversation from the financial page to the gossip column.

Nobody in our little enclave ever ventured much farther from home than to Doker for gas and groceries or to the Walmart at Bertrandville for larger purchases, unless they were making a beer run to a wet town across some county line or headed to the nearest hospital.

(Tiny and isolated as our "community" was, the Rushing Valley people still seemed to get up to regular excitement—Faith Sue and Jacob Wells were in constant domestic dispute and their twins, Isaac and Newton, were perpetually on the way to the emergency room at Northwest Arkansas Regional Medical Center; Malcolm was always falling in some hole and needing to be rescued; and I was . . . Well, I was in constant existential crisis— making the Rushing Valley, even small as it was, a microcosm of the world as much as anyplace else, I suppose.)

Malcolm did not like to get farther north than the store or farther south than the creek or go much beyond the hills that narrowly defined the Rushing Valley on the east and west. But he did once or twice a week have to drive Mean Joe's old Buick into Doker when the reverend needed something from town he didn't have at UPUMPIT!, like a fresh supply of live bait.

"Cricket s'posed to come in."

His granddad kept crickets in a ventilated plywood box in the back of the store and pint containers full of nightcrawlers in the Coca-Cola cooler. Fishermen on their way west to The Little Piney State Park bought them, occasionally.

I tapped the crystal of my watch again, but the sweep hand was not stirred. So, it would stay seven thirty-three, which would at least be accurate one more time that day. I finished my Coke, which was tepid already. The tranquilizers made me woozy.

"You see anybody strange around downtown lately?" I asked after a while.

Malcolm didn't answer.

"Well?"

"May be I did."

He looked off, avoiding my stare.

"You did."

Malcolm shook his head.

"Bible says not to tell a lie, Malcolm Ray."

"I know 'bout the Bible more'n you, Bob Reynold," Malcolm said, sore on this point with me. "Ain't telling no lie."

"Sin of omission," I said. "Leaving something out is just as bad as making something up." I did not believe this, but it was a useful axiom to weaponize on occasion against people who actually occupied and operated on moral high ground like Malcolm.

Malcolm glared at me.

"You tell me why you're calling up Sheriff—I tell you who I seen downtown," he bargained.

It would be common knowledge soon anyway, what I had found in The Little Piney.

"When I was taking my walk this morning I saw a man in the creek," I said. "Drowned."

Malcolm's jaw went slack. He held his breath.

"Who was it, Bob Reynold?"

"Big white man, maybe late thirties or forty years old. He had a Marine tattoo right about there on his arm."

I touched the kid's forearm and he jerked back, stepped away from the truck, looked up at the sky, let out a big halitosis sigh.

"Thank You, Jesus Rising Star," he whispered, clearly relieved, not talking to me.

I waited.

"Malcolm Ray? You know the fellow?"

"It wudn't my daddy," he said. "He ain't got no tattoo like that. His tattoos all ladies or monsters."

"Was the big, dead white man maybe who you saw downtown?"

The kid looked at me sideways.

"You seen him too, Bob Reynold." He said this as an accusation, so my stomach plonked into my groin.

I shook my head, no.

The kid shrugged.

"Like you say, Bob Reynold, not telling is just another way o' lying," Malcolm said, clearly pleased he'd turned the tables on me, but not rubbing it in. "And whichever way, it's a sin against Jesus."

"Where did you see this stranger, and what was he wearing?" I asked.

"All's I could see was he was wearing a red shirt and he was hanging out at the Old Lion."

"When?"

"One morning, couple of days ago, when I was down there acrossed the street in the Goody's Grocery Sto' parking lot, sitting in PaPaw's Buick, waiting on the first Trailways bus, waiting for the Grey's cricket." He paused and looked at me closely and then looked away, toward the store. "You know when it was 'cause you truck was parked right there on Ellum Street, Bob Reynold. Parked right behind those 'zalea bushes back of Miss Ollie's EAT place. Cantycornered from Miss TamFay's place."

"I wasn't in the truck," I said.

Malcolm shrugged.

"I thought you was in it with your 'noculars looking over at Miss TamFay's Old Lions."

"My pickup might have been there, Malcolm. Tammy Fay was working on the transmission and she might have parked it over there to clear some space in the garage. But you didn't see me in the truck," I insisted. "And you *did not* see any binoculars. I don't even own a pair of binoculars." I didn't anymore, at least.

Malcolm shrugged, looked off into the hazy blue sky.

"What day was that?" I asked.

He tugged on one of his outsticking ears.

"Day 'fore yesterday, I guess. Whatever day that was."

"Monday?"

"Sound right," Malcolm said. "S'posed to get cricket in on First Day of Week, but they didn't come in. This morning still ain't come in yet. Must be bad time for cricket raising, wherever they raise 'em at."

"What was the stranger doing," I asked, "at Tammy Fay's place?"

Malcolm cut his eyes at me and squinted, again.

"Parked up under the front shed, in a blood-color car . . ."

"Like a maroon-color sedan?" I asked.

"You always fixin' my words, Bob Reynold," Malcolm said and shrugged. "Look blood color to me. You need to 'pologize."

"I apologize," I said, meaning I apologized for my intrusive grammar and linguistic lessons since they consistently had absolutely no instructional efficacy whatsoever with my friend and so served no pedagogical purpose at all in our relationship and merely reflected the insistence of my own tastes in semantics.

Malcolm accepted my apology with his normal good nature.

"Thass all right, Bob Reynold."

"So, what was the man in the red shirt doing while he was sitting at the Old Lion in the bloodred car?"

"Just sitting there like he was waiting to get some gas, but it hadn't been no gas pumps there at the Old Lions in a long time and anybody can see that."

"The man in the car was a big man? How old would you say?"

Malcolm stretched an earlobe.

"Bigger'n you, Bob Reynold. Not old's you," Malcolm judged. "But he's a good-looking man and had a full head of hair and hairs all over his arm even where he had it danglin' out the car."

"And he wasn't doing anything? Spying on somebody or smoking or anything?"

"He look asleep to me," said Malcolm. "It's how I sleep in a car wit' my head back and mouth open. Flycatcher, PaPaw call me when I rest like that."

"And you didn't know him?"

"He wudn't nobody I know to name, I know that." Malcolm seemed certain of this uncertain identification.

"You didn't see him and Tammy Fay talking or anything?"

"Not just then, Bob Reynold. But that man he been around before. For some years, off 'n' on. Friend with Doc too, I think. Just I don't know him. He don't come in the sto' here." Malcolm jerked his head toward UPUMPIT! where his grandfather hovered just in the shade of the doorway, like a watchful shadow, then moved away out of sight.

This information from Malcolm seemed to complicate the situation for me. Malcolm continued.

"Some months back I seen him too with Miss TamFay arguing 'bout something," he said. "But not this time. This time I saw him lately he was just sitting in his car and then the bus pull into the grocery store parking lot and it wudn't any cricket, so I went on into Goody's Grocery Sto' and bought some those white cans for PaPaw and when I come out that blood-color car was gone."

"What's a white can, Malcolm?"

"Whatcha callit. 'Neric?"

"Generic," I supplied. That's what I bought too, generic cans and boxes of this and that, all packaged in white with black text describing contents simply as BEANS or MAC 'N' CHEESE or TOMATO SOUP. I was as cheap as Mean Joe, but with a lot less reason to be stingy that way.

I thought of what next to ask Malcolm, but he had a question for me.

"I think you ol' truck was gone too, from Ellum Street, wudn't it, Bob Reynold?"

I said nothing.

"Seems like before I went into Goody's Grocery I seen the bloodred car at Miss TamFay's Old Lions and I seen you truck behind the 'zalea bushes, but then when I come out of Goody's Grocery Sto' it's both them gone."

"I don't think that is correct, Malcolm. I don't believe my truck was downtown on that particular morning at all."

Malcolm stared at me with enough intensity to make me move. I slid off the tailgate of the truck, headed toward the store. Inside I saw no one but I could hear the chainsaw of Storekeep Pickens whining from somewhere nearby. I snagged the heavy fobbed key ring for the ladies' room off a nail in the wall, walked down a narrow aisle and out the back door, went around to the north side of the building, which was nearly covered in snakeskins tacked to the wooden walls, curing.

In the sideyard the rattlers in Malcolm's deep snake pit were entwinations of limp, overheated flesh. My stomach churned as I looked down at them and I wished Malcolm would hurry up and make of all those snakes the nice wallets they had taught him to make at Special School.

I locked myself into the restroom, the only cool, spotlessly clean place for miles around and started washing my hands.

Outside, Malcolm played a sweet old hymn on his harmonica.

The captive snakes were a sibilant, half-buried presence.

I threw up in the sink.

❧

Some minutes later Malcolm thumped on the frosted glass of the ladies' room door.

"Sheriff here, Bob Reynold."

I tapped powdered soap from the Borax dispenser, wet it with fulvous water, scrubbed my teeth with a finger end, swallowed the soap spit, double washed my hands, dried off with a roll towel, left the restroom, reentered the store by the back way, rehung the key ring.

Mean Joe Pickens Senior, the right reverend, was sitting on a low stool behind the zinc-topped counter, whittling a big crucifix cross out of osage orangewood. His clasp knife sliced through that branch of hardwood like through cardboard.

"Good morning, Reverend," I said.

Mean Joe did not look up from his handwork. His lap

was littered with curled shavings. His face in profile was a sharp-edged stone with blood vessels running under his pale skin like dirt veins shooting through quartz.

There was a deer rifle propped in a corner of the picture window behind him, a scruffy gray cat curled around the well-oiled stock. A bluebottle fly buzzed against the glass, slid down and up and side to side in a regular pattern until the cat killed it and swept it to the floor.

"That's one opinion," the preacher said, which was more than he usually said to me.

The reverend rose slowly, an engine of old repose cranking reluctant to some absolutely necessary action, every mechanism in him seeming stoved up from rust. He jerked his long chin at a paper chit pad on the countertop nearby a chewed-down pencil stub. He laid his crucifix cross on the countertop, laid his hands atop the splintered wood.

His hands were huge, hard as the hardwood beneath them, the gnawed fingernails the same color as that orangewood. An index finger tapped the decussation of the cross, about where the tortured head of Jesus might be hung.

"That's fifty cents for one Coca-Cola. And so for two is one dollar. Plus ten cent deposit on two bottles is a dollar and twenty cents. Plus Arkansas State sales tax."

He glared at me as at a man far fallen from grace.

"Plus it's the fifty cents charge for holding your mail."

I signed the chits as "R. R. Reynolds, MFA" just to irritate Mean Joe because I had once told him that acronym meant I had earned a Masters degree at Fucking Around. But Mean Joe liked my money well enough so he collected his credit vouchers and put them away in a pigeonhole on the side wall, returned to his seat on the low stool, recommenced his whittling.

I pushed the front screen door half open. There was a tan-and-white police car parked near my truck.

"You have a nice day, Reverend," I said over my shoulder.

"Too late for that," he replied.

I nodded, agreeing with him, stepped out of the building and into the sliver of awning shade, lingered there a few seconds to let my eyes adjust to the glare.

"Shut the door," Mean Joe said. "It's hot as hell out there already."

I let the screen door swing closed behind me and did step into a day hot already as pure hell.

CHAPTER 4

The sheriff stood behind the open door of his Tan-and-White. He adjusted his cowboy hat and nodded at me.

I started toward him, but Malcolm rushed up and blocked my way.

"Bob Reynold, you going down to the creek with the sheriff?"

The kid was agitated, bouncing from foot to foot.

"I suppose so," I answered.

The strap of his overalls slid off and I put it back in place.

"Something the matter with that?"

Malcolm glanced the way of the sheriff. The lawman stared at us but was too far away to hear us.

"You seen anybody down there lately, Malcolm? At the creek?"

"Nossir, Bob Reynold. Just them mean-spirited kids of Jacobswell, shooting at them wildcats down the bridge."

"You seen Jacob down there?"

"Not since a couple of weeks when he was electrocuting all the fish out of the water with his generator box, Bob Reynold."

"Nobody else?"

"Just you, Bob Reynold. They is nobody else. Community's gone. You know that well's me."

Rushing was gone, never to return. From my perspective this was a selling point.

"Collection plate so empty at church last Sunday we didn't get but four dollars and a dime offering. PaPaw said attendance so low down he was going to have to go to Li'l Rock to fetch some peoples in real need."

The kid was always hitting me up for money for his church but at Christmas I had donated five hundred toward paving their parking lot and had seen no asphalt spread, so I wasn't in the mood to be additionally charitable.

"I got things to do right now, Malcolm Ray. Why you holding me up?"

He kept bouncing and did not seem to be listening to me.

"You come on this Sunday, Bob Reynold. I'm doing Special Music."

I shook my head. I hadn't been inside a church since my momma's funeral. And I hadn't learned anything that bleak day, but that I was, truly, not a churched person.

"You like my daddy someways, Bob Reynold. You think the Lord He's abandoned you," Malcolm said quietly. "But ya'll got it backwards—it's ya'll abandoned the Lord Jesus Christ Rising Star, my daddy and Bob Reynold both. Times of trouble, when you be needing the Lord, the Lord might not know who Bob Reynold is."

The sheriff honked his car horn.

"I'll take my chances, Malcolm Ray."

I stepped around him, but the kid grabbed my arm, bent his head close to mine.

"Sheriff's looking for my daddy."

I stared hard at Malcolm. He didn't look away.

"Your daddy jumped bail some days ago, Malcolm Ray. You know about that?"

"Yessir."

"You know where he's at?"

The kid didn't blink. I blinked.

"Nossir, Bob Reynold. Figured you could find out if the sheriff know."

Baxter honked the cruiser's horn again. I lifted a hand.

"I got to go, Malcolm."

He nodded.

"I'll try to find out what the sheriff knows."

"I'preciate you, Bob Reynold."

I nodded, headed toward the lawman. Malcolm shuffled toward the store.

"And I pray for you to be in church on Sunday," he said so I could hear.

I looked backward to see Malcolm framed in the doorway of Pick's place, his granddad looming over him, both of them staring through the rusty, warped door screen at the law in their yard.

The tin roof of the store ticked with heat.

Malcolm lifted a hand at me. His PaPaw pulled him backward into the dark.

❧

I don't like cops. I don't like judges either, soldiers, Uniforms in general except for firemen.

It's a question of who should be in authority maybe. Maybe I think it ought to be me. Maybe I believe people in general should be more sensible and take care of their own troubles privately and then we all wouldn't need so much public policing. Maybe I just think the Law is generally useless for leveling things, that life is as corrugated, twisted and irregular as my bowel system and meant to be that way and if the fit survive they do for a reason but it's hard to tell by looking or the law who the fit are.

"You're Randy Reynolds," the cop, Baxter, told me.

He stood behind a decal of the encouraging phrase, TO SERVE AND PROTECT.

"Bob," I corrected, set a handshake in motion, but checked it when the sheriff stuffed his right hand into the pocket of his center-creased jeans.

With two fingers he tweezed out a government-green Zippo, pulled a pack of Camel shorts from the pocket of his starched white shirt, lit up a coffin nail. The stone in his thimble-size armed forces finger ring was blood red.

He was probably my age or thereabouts and only slightly taller than I was but he was a rock-hard if well-worn forty-something with a broken-in-boot face that remained rakish in an old-fashioned way. He had woman-size hands, as small as mine, but with a brawler's set of knuckles. His pure white summer-weight hat was about a six and three-quarters, spotless, pressed in a fashion favored by rodeo cowboys and dead movie stars.

"Sheriff Baxter," I said, completing our introductions.

Baxter nodded once then laid a hand on the ivory grip of his very big sidearm. Though we were about the same level of shortish, the sheriff looked hard and deadly as a rifle while I looked more like the scabbard for the rifle or, as my wife used to say of me, a sack of wet shit that needs to get dumped.

I sucked in my potbelly.

"We'll take my vehicle," he said, flicked his barely smoked cigarette on the ground. "Give us a chance to visit."

The smell of whitewashed drinking (mint mouthwash over hard liquor) was as unmistakable on him as it was familiar.

I stomped the smoldering cigarette.

"I'd rather drive my truck back home."

Baxter moved toward his driver's seat.

"I'd rather you didn't, Mister Reynolds."

He got in his cruiser, shut the door.

Mean Joe would have my truck towed as soon as I was out of sight. This had happened to me before. But Tammy's Towing Service needed the business and getting towed would give me a reason to get near her.

Malcolm banged out of the front door of the store, stuffing stick after stick of chewing gum into his maw, Juicy Fruit being the kid's tranquilizer.

"I'm riding with the sheriff, Malcolm," I raised my voice. "When Tammy Fay gets here with her tow rig, tell her to try to fix the transmission again."

Malcolm nodded.

His granddad appeared behind him. The deer rifle was in the reverend's hands and he rubbed the scarred stock with a red mechanic's rag.

I went around to the passenger side of the sheriff's cruiser, opened the door, sat down inside a cool, quiet place that smelled strongly of dead cigarettes and old, scared sweat, faintly of vomit and french-fried potatoes.

Baxter reversed us onto Poe County Road 615 without a backward glance, shifted into drive and accelerated down the road like he knew exactly where we were going.

We rode in silence, at a slow, even speed, for a couple of minutes, rolled past the Rushing Cemetery where sixty-four men and women and twenty-two children were buried—Duncans and Browns and Lewises and Wellses interred besides the McLahans, Smiths, Pickenses, Roberts and even the one Reynolds, one of my own old home folks, the single, solitary old bastard left around these

Ozark parts, before the rest of my paternal clan migrated into the Midwest and Texas.

"You got people up here," the sheriff said like he knew I did.

"From a long, long time back." I tapped on my closed window. "In the graveyard. Out there."

"There's a Robert Reynolds," Baxter told me what I knew already. "Born about the end of the War."

My paternal great-great grandfather, Robert Peter, had been born in a log cabin, in Rushing, in 1865, died in the same cabin twenty-eight years later of a ruptured liver and a gunshot wound in the back. His grandson had wildcatted the southern Arkansas and northeast Texas oil that eventually created the generational wealth that left me most of my modest little fortune.

I was surprised the sheriff was so familiar with the old headstones. But I was familiar with them as well.

"Is it your mother buried there?" I asked the sheriff.

I tapped on the window again, towards Frances Mary Baxter, dead six years and eight months, more or less.

"My mother was a Roberts," Baxter told me and seemed disinclined to tell me more.

"So, that's your mother buried in Rushing Cemetery?"

Baxter did not say yes and did not say no.

"Your daddy still alive?" I pressed.

Baxter shrugged then squinted, which I thought was an unusual gestural reply to that simple question. I did not pester him about his family as I did not like to get pestered about mine. The sheriff lowered his side window, tossed his live cigarette.

"High fire hazard out here now," I said, though every fool in the state of Arkansas knew this about that summer: red, white and black DANGER: NO OPEN BURNING signs were posted pretty much all over that droughty part of the country that summer.

Baxter raised his window, punched in the cigarette lighter on the dashboard, waited until it popped, then lit a fresh unfiltered, exhaled into the windscreen.

I coughed.

"Good fire clean this valley right out," he said.

We rode past other remnants of failed Rushing.

Point seven miles south of Mean Joe's current establishment of UPUMPIT! were the remnants of the original Pickens Family Mercantile Store now just three chisel-cut granite steps that led to a pile of weathered gray boards with nails in them like gunshot wounds bleeding rust. Nearby there four tarpaper shacks huddled together in an overgrown field where granite miners had once tried to eke a living out of the hills. The walls of these old hovels were collapsed by the load of their roofs and canted uniquely as each fought gravity from a different angle, but all were dedicated to the decomposition and disappearance of another failed, human venture.

"That's why you moved up here," Baxter told me.

I was not sure what he was talking about. I thought he would ask about the dead man. He didn't.

I shrugged.

"Family ties," he explained. "That's what brought you up here last year."

My twice great-grandfather, the last of the Reynoldses to die in Arkansases, was decomposed in a pine box in the unregenerate dirt of Rushing Cemetery; but that presence didn't seem much an enticement to relocate from the posh, Gulf Shore condo I had been in, moved into after my wife's death.

But I had never been comfortable in a condo—the carpet was always dirty and stained, the neighbors too loud, the parking lots around the place just heat collectors, the mailboxes jammed full of flyers for real estate and car washes and cheap furniture.

"Could not say what brought me up here," I admitted.

Rushing did not feel like Home. But you had to be somewhere and the persistent poverty of the place, the hard lines of the hills, the rocky fields that yielded little spoke, someway, to my condition, rose familiar in my impending middle ages from an artesian depth that my old home folks seemed preserved in.

I was newish rich now, living like old poor for reasons somewhat uncertain even to me.

"Who knows exactly what moves people to do what they do," I told the sheriff, something he knew already probably, that blood, a man's nature, is thick, runs deep, is hard to shake or slake and that life is too usually just about living, surviving somewhere or anywhere.

What was left of the old schoolhouse went by on the right. Jacob Wells had stripped it to a skeleton, relocated the dry-rotted wallboards to his place, piling the useless lumber between his collection of bald tires and his cadre of rusted-out propane tanks and his army of dysfunctional household appliances and log skidders, thrown a blue plastic tarpaulin over the worm-eaten planks, because that was my neighbor's fine idea of progress—to get whatever he could onto his dog-chewed piece of property and get a blue, plastic tarp over it.

"You don't get along with your neighbor, I hear," the sheriff said as we passed by the Wells place.

"The Twins shoot holes in my mailbox, shoot at my

truck, call me names. Jacob's dogs shit in my yard. His sheep and goats eat my garden. And I can't hardly leave my house without some Wells or another coming over and stealing whatever he or she can steal from my house. Jacob even stole the hay out of my field when I went off to Hot Springs for a weekend. Came in and cut it and baled it and moved it all out in two days."

Baxter grunted.

"I know what you're saying, Mister. Jake Wells was boxing the fox, stealing apples out of my daddy's orchard since he could walk. You move into country like this, though, you got to expect what you get."

"He's no account, as far as I'm concerned," I said. "And too stupid to drag a board around the house."

"Out here, Mister Reynolds," the sheriff advised me, "you just got to know who you're doing business with."

We passed the First Rushing Evangelical True Bible Prophecy Church of the Rising Star in Jesus Christ.

"You know the Reverend Pickens?" I asked.

"Mean Joe married my folks, buried my mother and baptized me," the lawman said.

Baxter didn't seem the baptized type.

"You know him and his grandson, the Retard, pretty good," Baxter said to me, pointedly I thought.

"I know his grandson, Malcolm, pretty good," I said.

"So I hear tell," Baxter said, as he braked in front of my place.

We sat the car for half a minute. I counted.

The sheriff didn't say anything, so I just waited, counted up and then counted down to calm my nerves.

"Malcolm's worried about his daddy," I said finally.

"He has got good reason to worry," the sheriff said. "Junior's jumped bail, which was the Reverend's last cash money lost. So if Mean Joe catches Junior he will surely tear his son a new asshole and then probably kill him outright." The sheriff paused, then added, "and the bondsman in West Memphis has set the hardest hard-case bounty hunter in Arkansas after Junior's ass besides."

"And you're after him too, Sheriff?"

Baxter looked at me.

"That goes without saying, Mister."

I fidgeted.

"You know where Joe Junior might be?" I asked for Malcolm's sake.

The sheriff cut his eyes at my house and raised his lip a fraction.

"You might want to check for him in a burn barrel, Mr. Reynolds. That's where trash usually winds up around here."

❧

I bought the Old Duncan Place because it was cheap property and a lot of it, but the house was a crooked, unrighteous mess. Clapboard peeled and bucked off the frame like dried-out scabs. The tin roof was streaked with deltas of rust. Thick coats of dust turned the windowpanes into privacy glass. My chickens moved listlessly on a front porch that was canted as a loading ramp, behind bug-screen wavy and patched with duct tape Xs.

The candy-apple red, fin-tailed Cadillac convertible I had bought my dead wife, a singular indulgence, a bribe, an investment, sat beside this wrecked abode like a reminder of better times.

It was so hard to explain to people why I lived this way

that I'd quit trying. Some of us were just not meant to enjoy money.

"Still got your Texas plates on the Caddy," Baxter noticed. "So you're not planning on staying around here then, I take it. Little slow out here for you, Mister Reynolds?"

I shrugged.

I had no idea whether I was leaving soon, or staying put for a while. That depended. I didn't like it here especially, but I didn't dislike it either. I had local interests. It was someplace to be.

Baxter drew hard on his cigarette, forced smoke out his nose, looked at me, at the house, at the Cadillac, then back at me. He shook his head as if all that did not add up. He chain lit another Camel, rolled down his side window and tossed the old butt on the road. That one cigarette, under the correct circumstances, could ignite a fire to burn my whole hundred acres, a thousand beyond, burn black the whole valley.

He rolled his window back up.

"You letting me out here?" I asked.

Baxter accelerated down the road.

"Seems you said he was down this way," the sheriff told me.

A hot bead of sweat slid down my spine, dripped off my tailbone.

"Did I?"

Baxter aimed his gray eyes at me, lifted that corner of his mouth again.

"I do believe it is what you said, Mister."

He sounded as if he was reminding me of a deal we had made a long time before.

"I suppose I said he was a 'he' too."

I stared at my little hands, swollen fat by the heat. I clenched and unclenched them, twisted the tight wedding band on the heart's finger of my left hand, felt a golden edge cut hard into the flesh between my knuckles, pressed my palm against my shirt front, felt the other wedding band, the dead man's property hanging there against my skin.

"I suppose you did say it, Mister."

I nodded, stared out my side window. Half a dozen of Jacob's sheep, shaggy and dirty as a junkie's hair-do, grazed in my front forty like it was common ground.

"He is down by the creek," I said. "I pulled him out of the water. He's on the northside bank."

We were near the bridge. Baxter slowed the cruiser to a crawl.

"He better be," the sheriff said. "Because I'd hate to come all the way out here for nothing."

It seemed though that he had.

The sheriff parked on the middle of the old bridge, but kept the cruiser's motor and the AC running. We got out and I moved to the side of the bridge that would give view to the dead man's resting place. The sheriff moved beside me, too close for comfort.

The body was gone.

Baxter sighed like he'd been holding his breath. His breath was like vaporized peppermint schnapps. He seemed relieved, but he could have been frustrated, hungover or something else. He was hard for me to read.

He stared at the north bank of The Little Piney where I was staring, spat cleanly over the rusted rail of the bridge into the water below. With a thumb he pushed up the brim of his hat, just a hair.

"He was right down there, Sheriff."

The white oak in the creek clung to land with thick

torqued roots. Green leafed, it was the livest plant around. Even the usually succulent kudzu vines were dry, fibrous as sisal rope wound around the trunks and limbs of heat-exhausted trees on the cut bank.

When I leaned against the bridge rail and pointed at the spot where I had found the corpse, the ring on the gold chain around my neck slid over the collar of my T-shirt.

The sheriff looked at the ring on the chain, not at where I pointed. He raised his eyebrows and frowned, which complex maneuver seemed the sort of facial move that lawmen must practice and which could mean anything from personal knowledge to professional curiosity. I tucked the chained gold band back under my shirt.

When I dropped my hand I felt sweat cold in my armpit.

"I suppose, Mister Reynolds," he said conversationally, "that a rich fellow from Houston and Gulfport and wherever else you been, would just naturally get bored living out in this kind of Pure Country."

The sheriff had checked up on me.

"I don't think you understand Rural America. How it is out here."

Though the High Sheriff might have been aiming at informed sarcasm, his critique came off as canned. And he was clearly underinformed about me on these older counts, since I'd been born in a town not much bigger than Doker and raised in one no bigger than Bertrandville and only lived in Houston because that was the only place that would accept me in graduate school and only had traveled some of the world because my father drug me on business trips around the world only to carry his bags and tend to him when he was drunk, which my mother would not do for her husband.

But I didn't say anything. People think they know you when they know where you're from or where you've lived or where you went to school or who your people are; but that is often not the case in the least bit and apples can roll as far from the trees that bore them as the grocery store, oftentimes many states and even countries far away from their place of origin.

The sheriff turned back to his car.

"Shouldn't we take a look?" I asked, because I felt I should ask, though I did not want to take a look with the sheriff.

It was curious that the body was back in the creek or gone elsewhere, but I was relieved that it was.

The sheriff made a big production of looking east and west and north and south.

"Take a look at what, Mister?"

Truthfully there was not much to see. Even the heel marks my walking shoes had made in the creekside mud seemed now smoothed to inconsequence.

I looked over the bridge rail. In the shallow water river stones were smooth and speckled as cresting trout, metal pull tabs glittered like silver jewelry, plastic bobbers were hooked in a nest of fishing line. A faint scent of burned wood rose as a quick hot breeze whisked up and twirled the white trash ash inside a fire pit like insubstantial egg whites, shirred to the ultimate thinness of dust. Empty cans of potted meat-food product and oysters, soda cracker wrappers and chewing gum wrappers and Styrofoam worm containers, beer cans and fish bones and heads, spent rifle cartridges littered the ground.

A branch snapped on the southside bank and the red-tailed hawk was yanked off his regular perch atop the loblolly and reeled into the blue sky.

I peered into the brush below the pine trees.

A feral cat showed itself. This was one of the tribe of housecats gone wild that inhabited all the area around the creek. The old yellow tom twisted his head skyward, looking up at the bird settled back in the loblolly. But the aerie of the hawk was a long climb up a tall tree for an unlikely meal, so the scroungy cat backed out of sight.

"I'm leaning towards just chalking this little episode up as a waste of County time, Mister Reynolds."

"Chalking it up," I repeated.

I wasn't complaining, though chalking it up did not sound like exactly correct procedure.

"I guess I could haul you in," the sheriff said casually, giving me the distinct impression that Sam Baxter did not like me, nor dislike me, but was, in actual fact, trying to figure out what to do with me.

"Haul me in for what, Sheriff?"

"I'm sure I could think of something, Mister Reynolds. I am High Sheriff of Poe County."

He moved toward the cruiser.

"Is that the way things work out here, Sheriff?"

He appeared to seriously consider that question.

"I'd have to say, yes, Mister. Things do work about like that out here."

He stared at me and his thin lips curled up, ever so slightly.

I blinked, brushed dust out of my eyes. I have a problem keeping my eyes open when someone stares at me.

"I didn't invent the man." I declared this with some surety, but I was not sure how sure I was about that. Pretty sure, I thought. But you never know.

I was reassuring myself more than arguing, but the sheriff took the opportunity that presented itself.

"So you say, Mister Reynolds," said the sheriff.

He sounded skeptical, as if I was not a credible witness in this case.

"Why would I?"

"That's the Sixty-Four Dollar Question, isn't it, Mister?" he said. "Why did you?"

"He was there," I said and nodded at the creek. "I don't know who he was or how he got there. But he was there."

Baxter thumbed loose tobacco off his lip. He did not act like he believed me.

"So you say. But you could have invented him, from what I hear tell of you, Mister Reynolds."

"What's that supposed to mean?"

The sheriff walked to the driver's side of the car, rolled up his shirtsleeves and laid his hands on the roof. His shirt was sweat-stained under the arms. The five-pointed star on his breast pocket was shiny brass.

A crude tattoo on the inside of his right forearm seemed familiar—an eagle, a banner, an encouraging, inspired motto.

"It means, Mister, that I heard you got a screw loose."

I stared at the spot where my dead man had been.

"Depends on who you talk to," I said.

"Well, Mister I believe you're right in saying that. In general. But when there's near about unanimous agreement on a man's state of mind, that saying kind of loses its punch, doesn't it?"

I spit, meaning to hit the water, but my spit dribbled onto my chin. I swiped at it with my hand.

"You don't know anything about me."

Baxter tapped on the roof of his car with the Zippo.

I turned around and he stared at me until I blinked.

"I know what I know," the sheriff said.

If he'd called the Houston Police Department he knew

that some homicide detectives there believed that if I had not exactly killed my wife I had had some hand in her death. Or rather, that I had failed to raise a helpful hand.

My wife possessed a lot of troubles from the start—drugs, men, women, whatever. After the miscarriage she just got worse, fell completely off her rocker, spent my money like crazy, on dope, on her people. My ex-in-laws, their lawyers, their private investigator, my lawyers, the insurance investigators, my distant relations all knew I'd been in therapy over all that, had never actually received a clean bill of mental health. But having an unclean bill of mental health is not a crime, yet and truth is hard to ascertain sometimes.

Though I was off serious medications Dr. Doc still mildly tranquilized me for my "nerves." I didn't usually talk much about my family affairs to strangers.

Jacob Wells and his ill-bred brood would say I was a crazy eccentric nuisance who threw rocks at their livestock.

Preacher Pickens, I was quite sure, despite my charitableness to his church and the fact that I paid his grandson ten dollars a week to, basically, do nothing, considered me a bad influence on his grandson Malcolm.

Baxter grinned the sort of grin the cat gets when it gets the canary in the coal mine, just before the bird squawks.

I wanted to drop him in a very deep hole and dump snakes on his head.

"You don't know shit," I said, looked away before another staring match ensued.

Baxter sniffed and wiped a hand over his chin in another gesture that seemed well rehearsed.

"Well, Mister, let me just put it to you like this—if a dead man, a dead drowned man, does show up in this creek, anywhere within hailing or driving distance from your domicile . . ."

He let that veiled threat curtain between us for a moment.

I stared at the water.

"Your wife drowned, didn't she," Baxter stated, didn't ask. "Official cause of death was drowning."

The Little Piney was moving under me. I felt dizzy.

"My wife was a drug addict, Sheriff. She fell asleep in the bathtub."

I saw, I imagined her face in the creek below me, her blue eyes open, her blond hair spread, darkened in the water as a nun's black habit.

"She drowned," Baxter reminded me again, lowered his voice. "And she had thumb marks on her neck and bruises on her shoulders."

She was very frail. Still beautiful, but very frail by then, junkie thin, with papery, pale skin that bruised easily.

When I'd lifted her out of the tub she'd been light in my arms as an underfed child.

"Yes, Sheriff. The official cause of death was accidental drowning."

My lawyers had persuaded for that grand jury verdict four years and three months before. I was the older, parsimonious, boring husband of a very attractive, very unstable young woman, but there was no evidence to indict me for any wrongdoing.

I was a good husband.

If it was a suicide, she hadn't left me a note. But that was no surprise to anyone. My wife had never thought much of me and had been pretty public about that disregard.

"She did drown," I repeated, so there would be no confusion.

It was as easy for me to understand how I lost her as it had been difficult for me to understand how I got her. Even with my money, I was not the kind of man to get a woman like that—not for long, not for keeps.

Baxter studied me for a moment, lifted an eyebrow,

tossed his straw Stetson through the open door of the cruiser.

He had a full head of short-cropped salt-and-pepper hair.

"I hear your daddy drowned too. That right, Mister Reynolds?"

"In a manner of speaking, Sheriff," I allowed.

I was still living at home then, almost twenty-five years old, taking care of my invalid mother. I found him collapsed in his car, Jim Beam in hand.

"He choked to death on his own vomit," I recalled, wiped the sweat sheen off the bald spot at the back of my head.

Baxter nodded.

"He was a chronic alcoholic, Sheriff. An affliction I'm sure you're familiar with."

I knew that was pushing it, but I was mad.

Baxter just narrowed his eyes.

"Your mother managed to die of natural causes, I hope, Mister Reynolds."

I nodded.

My mother followed her husband into the grave pretty much, pausing only long enough to put her strange affairs in order. Codependents my parents would be called currently, though not, perhaps, in most conventional senses were they . . .

Enablers.

As they did not really enable each other, but quite the opposite. They, sort of, eventually, killed one another.

That was another one of their mistakes I had not repeated. I had not let my wife kill me.

"Heart failure," I said.

It had always been my understanding that Momma loved me like she did him, but her sudden departure from my continuing scene led me to believe otherwise. She did leave me most of her money, which had been my daddy's money, which had been his daddy's money. But she allowed me my full inheritance, one hundred percent, only after I swore on one of her many Holy Bibles to keep her storefront church open . . .

Which I did not do.

Because I do not, really, believe in Promises.

Semper Fi, you can have it.

"My momma died in the hospital," I said.

Baxter nodded, as if he knew that that was a lie from me even though he was not sure because he had not done that much background check on me.

Actually, my mother had died at home with me in the house. She had a heart attack and drowned facedown in her oatmeal bowl.

The sheriff looked over my shoulder at the fenced-in "compound" over on the south side of The Little Piney, then he looked back at me, stared at me.

"You know what 'modus operandi' is, Mister?"

"It's the way a fella has of doing something that is peculiar to that particular fella," I answered. "More or less."

"So . . . ," he said, hitched up his pistol-weighted belt. "Let's just say if a man does turn up dead by drowning nearby, you're going to be first on my list of prime suspects for putting him there, Mister Reynolds. So if I was you, I'd forget about this particular fantasy of yours of finding a dead man in The Little Piney right here."

"All right," I said, not looking his way, looking at the creek, right at the spot where I knew I thought I'd seen the dead man, "Buck."

"And, out of courtesy, Mister Reynolds, I will remind you once more that I'm High Sheriff of Poe County. And ask you plainly if you get my drift about what that might mean for you."

I nodded. "I get your drift, Sheriff Baxter," I said, because I did.

"Just a word to the wise, Mister."

"I got it," I said. "High Sheriff," I repeated. "Poe County. Word to the wise should be sufficient."

"We're on the same page so far, Mister Reynolds."

If the High Sheriff of Poe County and I were on the same page that would be the first time in a long time I had been on the same page with anybody, so I doubted that we really were. But I did not argue with Sam Baxter about where we were relative to one another. The High Sheriff of Poe County was not someone I wanted to arrest me or book me, and I surely did not want to become to him any sort of Person of Interest.

Sheriff Sam Baxter got in his car, shut the door, backed off the bridge, turned the Tan-and-White around in County Road 615 and drove east in a cloud of red dust.

He didn't ask me if I wanted a ride.

I wouldn't have taken it anyway.

CHAPTER 5

I stood on the bridge, blinking. According to my dead watch it was seven thirty-three and would be forever if I kept that watch on.

I slipped the cheap Timex off my wrist.

I'd worn a watch, every day and every night, since I was in grade school, usually a cheap Timex, so without a watch on my wrist my whole arm felt strange, even more insubstantial than as per usual.

But maybe it was time to quit keeping time and quit worrying so much about dead bodies and such.

I had the unsettling feeling that the lawman Baxter did not much appreciate me ruining his morning with what he perceived to be a false alarm and that he and I had business as yet unfinished; but I was tired of keeping track of who I had business with, quick and dead.

I threw the wristwatch as far upstream as I could and watched the cheap piece of plastic float almost instantly under the bridge.

But maybe I was imagining the sheriff's rancor toward me. I had been accused of paranoia before, officially and unofficially.

And I should have had something better to do with my time than stand on a bridge in a backwater of northwest Arkansas wondering why a local county sheriff had gone to the trouble to make general inquiries of me and lower my self-esteem.

But I didn't.

Apart from my garden and my chickens nothing in the world depended on me in the slightest. Even my money took care of itself, multiplied even as I stood staring down at water that appeared deep and cool but was really not much deeper at its deepest than a tall man standing and was as warm along the edges as blood.

I thought of what to do.

Do Nothing made a very persuasive argument. Most of my life I usually Did Nothing, so it was a familiar activity I was successful at.

I was probably in trouble already.

County Road 615, as a maintained public road, terminated at the old iron bridge.

I strolled to the south side of the bridge and examined tire tracks in the dust of what CR 615 continued to be past its legally maintained limits.

No matter my other flaws, I will say I am rather meticulous in my observations.

(There are seventy-six teeth on one side of the zipper of my favorite short pants, for instance. Thirty-five nylon bristles per tuft on my toothbrush, forty tufts, fourteen hundred bristles altogether.)

I noticed one particular set of tracks that ran under the gate of the fenced field and aimed south at the empty stone house one way and in a vaguely southeasterly direction down the rutted two-track road into the deep woods another way, all headed away from Civilization (as we knew it locally, at least).

I handled the pair of padlocks on the gate. Two locks on two chains. One chain on the ground.

There had always been three rusty locks on three lengths of rusted chain. I searched in the weeds until I found the third lock, in a mole hole, under a leaf, a rusty affair, sheared in two, by a small explosion probably, so not bulletproof as advertised. Then I noticed that the locks remaining on the gate were new, still slick with packing grease.

Somebody had shot the old padlocks off the gate, replaced two of them with new locks. Somebody in a hurry to get inside or somebody not supposed to be inside.

Behind me brush rustled. I threw a rock, more or less across the road in the general direction of the brush rustling.

"Let that one be a warning!"

I picked up another rock, one with better balance, I hoped.

Briefly a pale face appeared under a tree limb. The face was vaguely familiar.

"Hello?!" I yelled.

The face disappeared.

"I know it's somebody over there," I said, in a more conversational tone, I hoped. I was not a threat to anybody at that moment and did not want anyone to be defensive toward me.

It wasn't the dead man over there: that I was sure of.

"Mr. Pickens?" I guessed. "Are you Joe Pickens Junior?"

Nothing.

"I'm a friend of your boy's," I said. I don't know why I was proceeding, why I just didn't leave—maybe I stayed to settle something, find out something, maybe just to do something. Maybe to find Malcolm's daddy for him. "I'm a friend of Malcolm Ray's," I repeated, louder. "You can trust me," I promised.

I waited. A while.

"I'm not just going away," I said.

A man cleared his throat.

"Boy told me who you is, but I ain't trust nobody."

"Mr. Pickens? Joe Pickens Junior?" I asked.

Though I was pretty sure now who the man hiding by the creek was, if not where he was or what he meant to do.

"I don't mean you no harm, Man," he said. "So don't throw no more rocks."

"I apologize," I said. "It was an accident."

"Best not be no mo' accident again, Man, or I will fetch you up for reckoning."

That sounded like something the Right Reverend Pickens, Mean Joe, would say to Malcolm when he was mad at him.

"You don't have a gun, do you, Mr. Pickens?"

I had been beaten plenty of times, from forever, for reasons various and sundry, some probably justified, but I'd never been shot.

"I wished I did have a gun. But I ain't. Whoever told you that was lying."

"Nobody told me anything," I said.

I stepped toward the road.

"Don't come up on me, Man," Joe Junior warned. "Just because I ain't got no gun don't mean I ain't armed."

There was a flash of shiny metal in the brush that could have been a soda can, but also could have been a knife.

"All right," I said and showed my empty hands to any part of the world that could see them.

I had never been seriously cut before either.

Nothing more was said for over a minute. I counted.

"You Bob Reynold, what the boy call you," Malcolm's daddy said.

"That's right, Mr. Pickens."

"I know about you, Man. I know you name. The boy he keep care you chicken he said."

"That's right, Mr. Pickens."

"But you some older'n what the boy say. The boy he ain't right though. You see that."

"Malcolm's a good boy, Mr. Pickens. I never met a better kid. You're very lucky to have him as a son."

"Shit," Malcolm's daddy said.

I waited.

The man in the bushes cleared his throat.

"He ain't right. Fool could see that from day one."

"I imagine that's more your fault than Malcolm's, Mr. Pickens."

"His momma's fault, you mean," Joe Pickens Junior said. "That woman she a parking lot 'ho and a drunk to boot. You know about that?"

"I heard it of her," I said, though I had not heard this from her son, Malcolm, who thought she had gone off to make some money so she and he could have a house, with a yard and pit for his snakes and maybe even a swimming pool in the backyard.

"Woman she got some sort a blood defection now lately," Joe Pickens Junior said of his wife. "She be dead shortly, what I heard."

"That happens sometimes when people have unprotected sex with people they don't know about, Mr. Pickens. You could be infected too," I added.

"Huh? What you say, Man?"

"Nothing," I said. "Just a science lesson, Mr. Pickens."

I gathered myself. Malcolm's momma was dying of

AIDS, probably, the boy's daddy was hiding out from the Law in bushes alongside a nowhere creek at the end of a dead-end road . . . but there was a reward for Joe Pickens Junior. If I could bring him in, that reward would be mine.

"I'm just wondering what will happen to Malcolm if you get put in jail for a long time," I said. "If you come with me and turn yourself in it might go better on Malcolm," I suggested. "He's worried about you, Mr. Pickens. Your boy is worried about you."

"Hell," said Joe Pickens Junior. "That boy don't know what he's saying half the time and don't know where he is half the time and don't know what he is or what he thinking *all* the time. I never seen a thing like that boy. How you gone live with something like that as your own boy, Man? He plain stupid, Malcolm is."

"Malcolm's not the one hiding in the bushes though, Mr. Pickens."

Joe Pickens Junior didn't have anything to say about that judgment for a spell; but then he asked, "You got kids, Man?"

"No."

"Then shut up talking about them."

I sighed.

The stupidest, most worthless people in the world could have children and know more than I did just because I didn't have children and they did.

"What you bring Law down here for, Man? That's exactly what I want to know 'bout," Joe Pickens Junior said. "The boy tell you I was down up in here?"

"Malcolm didn't tell me a thing except he was worried about his daddy, Mr. Pickens. I just heard at the bar in Bertrandville that you had jumped bail and that the Law was interested in seeing you and bounty hunters after you. Since I know this was your old neighborhood, I just guessed it was you in the bushes," I said. I waited. "I swear, Mr. Pickens, it was just a guess it was you down here hiding out."

"So you brought Law down here to see 'bout me."

"Nossir. Like I told you, I didn't even know you were here, Mr. Pickens. Until just now, until you admitted yourself. I'm a friend of Malcolm Ray's. I wouldn't go against him."

"You a friend of the boy's don't make you no friend a mine, Man."

"Me bringing the sheriff down here had nothing to do with you, Mr. Pickens. We were together down here on an unrelated matter. I swear to that."

"You can swear to a lot o' things," said Joe Pickens Junior. "But you done did said one thing right, Man—it ain't got nothing to do with me. No, none a' this shitbidness on this creek and none of it over in there acrossed that cyclone fence got a thing to do with me, Man, an' surely never did."

"What business is that, Mr. Pickens?" I asked.

"Crazy-ass shit, Man," he told me.

"Did you see something down here lately? By the creek? Did you see somebody do something? Did you see somebody drive through the gate?"

"It ain't none a' my business one way or the other, Man. It's them's business. Sure somebody else's, not mine's. I didn't see nothing. I didn't do nothing. So, I ain't got nothing to say about it. None of this crazy-assed business is mine."

I could sense him moving downstream, our visit done. I had questions. But Joe Pickens Junior had more compelling reasons to leave than to stay and answer them.

"You tell the boy, stay 'way," he called to me.

I heard him splashing through shallow water and so I hurried to the bridge, looked over the eastside railing and saw Joe Pickens Junior slog through mud, gain a gravel shoal, turn around a bend. He was dressed neck to ankle in prison denim and there was a big butcher knife in his right hand and a plastic grocery bag in the other. I called after him, but Joe Junior did not look back. Not once. The fugitive just ran, like a rabbit without options. And he would have taken a bullet in the back without even looking at who shot him.

When Joe Pickens Junior—Malcolm's daddy, Mean Joe's son, somebody's estranged husband, many people's dope dealer—was long gone I strolled down the fence line that bordered the weedy twenty acres, glancing occasionally at the stone house in the near distance. Posted on the fence, every twenty feet, was a NO TRESPASSING: NO ENTRANCE WITHOUT WRITTEN PERMISSION OF THE OWNER: ALL VIOLATORS WILL BE PROSECUTED TO THE FULL EXTENT OF THE LAW sign. Between these signs, as evenly spaced, were signs that read HIGH FIRE DANGER: NO OPEN BURNING.

I kicked the bottom of the fence. It was buried in the dry dirt.

But thirty paces from the gate, I stumbled into a hole and discovered a jagged cut in the chain link—an egress, low down.

A two-foot-deep trench had been gouged out, and the buried fence pulled from the ground, the pencil-lead-thick wires of the chain-link fence crudely sheared. This entrance-exit was camouflaged with leaves and sticks. I removed the old-fashioned clothespins that held the steel curtain together, looked around, considered.

The corpse in the creek had not walked to the creek. No white man around there would walk as far as town to The Little Piney even for free money. So the way I saw it, the man I was calling Buck had either driven to the creek of his own volition or had been driven there—in his maroon sedan or in someone else's vehicle. If he had driven to the creek in his own car, then he was at least alive when he arrived at The Little Piney. But if he'd been driven to the creek, then he was either under serious duress— unconscious from a blow to the head, for instance—or else he was DOA at The Little Piney. A man that big would have to be pretty much out of it to be manhandled into the creek, even by another big man.

If Buck had driven to the creek, then I was probably in the clear.

But if he had been hauled to The Little Piney uncon- scious from a previous blow to the head and then dumped by party or parties unknown, well, then . . .

I wasn't sure what Malcolm had seen downtown Mon- day morning.

Probably nothing. If something not much. A scuffle in the gloomy wee hours under the portico of the Old Lion. A small man sneak-attacking a much bigger man as the big man lay sleeping in his sedan. Little man driving away from the scene in a beat-up pickup truck like mine.

I wanted to know if the maroon sedan Malcolm was calling "blood-colored" was around, parked in the woods or parked and hidden behind the high chain-link fence. Because if it was, then it was probable that the stranger, Buck, if that was, had been his name, had recovered from our very brief tussle on Elm Street, no real harm done him.

But why had he driven then to The Little Piney? To wait

for me? To ambush me during my morning constitutional and pay me back for beaning him, for blindsiding him while he stalked the woman I was trying to stalk? To scare me away from Tammy Fay for good? To maim me? To kill me?

Or had Buck been at The Little Piney looking for a bail-jumper, trying to recapture Joe Pickens Junior for a nice reward?

If the maroon sedan was parked around The Little Piney somewhere, then I probably hadn't killed the dead man and had nothing to worry about, since hitting a man who was spying on a female friend of yours (coshing him while he dozed with a very nice pair of Bushnell binoculars) was probably just a misdemeanor in Arkansas if you had the right lawyers and, even though Arkansas was not my natural home state, I imagined I would have the best lawyers available since the Land of Opportunity runs mostly on money just like every place else in the world.

But if Buck's car had been parked nearby, accessibly, and if Joe Pickens Junior had killed Buck and pushed him into the creek, then it seemed to me that such a nefarious criminal as that would not have hesitated to steal a car for his getaway. Joe Pickens Junior had not taken an abandoned maroon sedan, I was quite sure of that. If he had killed Buck, even Joe Pickens Junior wouldn't be stupid enough to be hiding in the bushes right at the crime scene on The Little Piney.

So, I ruled out Joe Pickens Junior as the killer of the man in the creek.

But he might very well have seen who did kill Buck or know what had happened to Buck.

It would be illuminating to speak more with Joe Pickens Junior.

Movement nearby the stone house caught my eye. I squinted and imagined a man.

"Mr. Pickens!" I yelled.

The figure blended into the slanted shadows against the south wall of the house.

I squinted harder. Maybe Joe Pickens Junior was hiding out in the abandoned stone house behind the cyclone fence.

"Mr. Pickens!" I yelled again. "Is that you?"

I waited for one minute then I parted the chain link and crawled into the weedy field. Plowing into waist-high Johnsongrass like a vertical lawnmower, I made my way to the stone house.

❧

The stone house was various shades of red and brown, sandstone and red rock, the cement between the field-stones highlighted by a sun straining toward midmorning.

Beside the house I saw what I thought was a man in dark pants, a red shirt and an orange cap. He seemed to turn my way, then froze like a spotlighted deer when he saw me, then collapsed like he was playing possum. I squeezed my eyes tight shut, reopened and refocused hard but the world to my myopic eyes remained blurry, smeared in the middle and only clear in my peripheral vision.

The stone house was eighty yards away. That was a long way for me to see with distinction anything as small as a man.

I needed my binoculars but they were long gone.

The field grass stirred, then stilled.

"Mr. Pickens?" I yelled, thinking that that man,

redressed, had backtracked, gone around the creek's bending and to ground inside the fenced area.

"Mr. Pickens?"

I waited, counted to calm myself. I didn't see anyone and probably hadn't seen anyone.

I went on, tripped and fell and my shoulder slammed into a half-rotted stump. I groaned and got up, took a few more steps toward the house and stumbled on another tree stump, the ordered remnants of an orchard.

On the weedy, crushed-rock driveway I paused.

"Hello, house!"

I could see clear to the backyard of the place, could see the corner of a detached garage and part of another out-building. I didn't see anybody, but I was not sure I wanted to see anybody.

The fine hairs on the back of my neck were raised though.

A pair of mangy feral housecats slunk across the drive-way and back into the weeds.

I counted again, but since this trick was not working to reduce my stress I went on. Cautiously.

"Hello? Anybody home here?"

A breeze blew hot across me, vaporized the sweat on my forehead and bald spot. I thought I heard the sound of a car coming from the dirt road that ran southeasterly into the deep woods. This road was only twin tracks gouged into red clay, virtually unpassable by anything other than an ATV during wet season, and still three miles of bad road to pavement even during dry season. I strained my ears but the sound of a motor was extinguished by the wind in the trees.

The grass was beaten down somewhat around the fieldstone building, a place that was not as pretty up close as from the road, with the slate roof gapped and chipped and the wooden window sash droopy and dry-rotted.

Dry leaves were piled up against the house like combustible brown snow. I smelled gasoline and another smell, like ammonia, cat piss.

The place seemed deserted by all but the feral felines. There were cats on the roof and cats in the trees and cats supine and cats mobile. Cats around like they owned the place. Most bolted when they saw me, some stayed put.

The sideyard was littered with disintegrating wooden bushel baskets, some with crenelated apples still in them. Pine needles clustered on the small slab porch. The varnish was worn off the front door. A hasped padlock, as old and rusty as the ones on the gate, kept out visitors.

I knocked, didn't wait but a moment before stepping into the sideyard where a rusted-out wheelbarrow was full of dried cat shit. On that southside wall of the house were two windows.

Between those two dark windows was an ornamental bush, a shoulder-high shrubbery, powdered thick with red dust, with a filthy, blaze-orange watch cap set atop it, probably the figure, the "man" I thought I'd seen.

I strained to see into the house, but all the glass was painted on the inside solid black.

I whirled around at a snaky hiss. A giant yellow tomcat glared at me from his crouched position on the edge of the sideyard. He bared his teeth, hissed again.

"Scram!"

I feinted a leap at him, but the cat just laid his ears flat, eyeballed me, rigid as a yellow-streaked stone.

As I stooped to pick up a slate shard the tom bounded and I discovered myself recoiled in the dusty shrubbery, put down by a raggedy housecat, which did not presage much good luck for this venture.

Spooky cat bastard.

I extracted myself from the decorative shrubbery. My

heart was racing. The giant tom was gone, so I threw a chunk of granite at some other cat, then patted my pants clean.

More broken bushel baskets littered a backyard hard-packed, unvegetated and covered with cat crap in various stages of dehydration.

In a lightning-scarred oak tree several more cats lounged, limp in the heat, draped over thick limbs like furred and whiskered sacks of soft bones.

Hanging by fishing line from the lower branches of the giant white oak were numerous rusted, perforated cans, many of them cat food–size. Some of the larger ones had bones in them as clappers. When the wind blew, the cans clanked together hollowly as the finger-long bones chimed dryly.

The Wells kids must have sawed the hole in the fence and turned the deserted place into their private play-ground. I couldn't imagine Isaac and Newton feeding cats though. The Wellses were Dog People if ever there were.

It could have been Malcolm too, I supposed, but Mal-colm claimed he wouldn't go across The Little Piney for penny biscuits and free gravy, because the place was haunted and because his grandfather forbade it for rea-sons unclear.

When I stepped up on the back slab porch a trio of mot-tled kittens tumbled off and away as if their back ends were not properly attached to their front ends. The win-dow glass of the door was painted solidly secret. I contin-ued into the backyard where there was a detached garage.

Fairly fresh tire tracks ran under what seemed incon-gruously to be a fairly new single-piece rolling garage door, which was padlocked tight to a thick iron ring set in a cement slab that also looked much newer than the rest of the construction around the place. One of the high, narrow windows of this garage door was cracked though, a sizable corner of a pane missing. But I was too short to see in.

There was nothing in the yard to stand on but rotten bushel baskets. The wheelbarrow, when I pushed it, fell apart like a prop in a comic sketch.

Behind the garage was another shed, its door hanging open. I peered inside and saw an old generator, cobweb shrouded and dusty, and several 55-gallon metal drums. The place smelled strong of gasoline and motor oil.

Next to the generator was a horizontal propane tank. Though the gauge on the tank was broken the eight-foot-long steel can still smelled of rotten eggs.

Atop this tank were two empty Coca-Cola cans with rough-edged holes punched in them to make rustic lanterns. The candles in them had reduced to pools of wax with nipples of charred wick. The top of a propane tank didn't seem a safe place to light votive candles. It seemed a queer place for a shrine, but it seemed a shrine.

Between the candleholders seven locks of braided hair, short as a thumbnail and delicately knotted, were arranged around a small mammal's skull.

I was in a feline shrine.

The close space smelled of burnt hair and, unmistakably, of a man, of dirty skin long cured in sweat, of rank, bare feet.

Sweat dripped off my tailbone.

I edged to the door of the shed, leaned out slightly.

The color red streaked by my face and my legs collapsed just before the heat and blackness spread over my brain and I fell.

CHAPTER 6

I woke up with a terrible headache.

In jail.

Hanging on the bars of an adjoining cell was a reedy man with neat, high-piled hair who massaged his crotch in a manner more habitual than provocative.

There was no other visible presence in the cell block.

"What you in for, Pard?"

My neighbor was lily white with purple skin hung up under his deep-set eyes like colostomy bags half filled with old blood. His scent was strong and complex—snuffed tobacco, fish guts, hair oil and expensive cologne, all lightly liquored up. His clothes were dirty, but his hands and fingernails were very clean.

I sat up on the edge of the cot, felt nauseated.

"You didn't answer my question right away, Pard."

His drawl was so cellular it was a speech impediment.

"Are you a character?" he asked me.

"Where am I?" I asked, to begin with.

"Poe County Jailhouse, Pard. Bertrandville, Arkansas, United States of America. You was in here when I got my own accommodations, so I am a little bit uninformed about you."

He stared at me, licked his lips like he was tasting old dinner.

"Are you the murderer, Pard?"

I almost threw up.

"Who said I was?" I managed to ask.

"All's I heard when Deputy Lloyd booked me was Sheriff found a floater in The Little Piney. Maybe murdered. And I just bet you know something about that, Pard."

My neighbor squinted at me, sneezed.

My empty stomach clenched against nothing. I was speechless.

"Been in here a awful lot," the fellow told me, sneezed again. "But ain't seen no murderer yet to tell of, so this will be a particular first."

He sneezed again, wiped his nose with a tattooed hand, grinned at me, sniffed.

The police had let him keep his jewelry on and the stone in his gold finger ring glowed blood red. One of his tattoos was of an eagle rampant.

I examined what I could see of the ceiling, then stared at the floor.

My neighbor hacked up a spoonful of phlegm and hocked it on the floor of my cell.

"Ain't a summer cold just the worse thing in the world, Pard?"

"I'm not a murderer," I said.

My neighbor was not relieved to hear this.

"Now that's a damned shame."

He swung on the bars between us like a bored monkey.

"Because a murderer would keep me entertained, I really figure one would." He sighed. "But it's no really good diversions for the truly evil wicked like us, is it, Pard?"

It seemed to me that there were plenty, but maybe I was wrong.

"You know what time it is?" I asked.

"'Bout couple hours or so after lunchtime, Pard, because we have done had our lunch a while back, us that wasn't beauty sleeping their lives away."

I felt a lump on the back of my head.

"Do you have any idea why I'm in here?"

"Nope, Pard, but I do know a good joke about three queer Jew doctors and a nigger hitchhiker, my neighbor told me. You ever heard a that one?"

"I made that one up," I said.

"Why, Pard, you're a funny man. I been looking for you. You and me's like-minded, like they say."

It was hard for me to argue that right then.

"I've got no sense of humor at the moment."

I felt like I had been drugged.

"I can't hardly believe that, Pard, to hear you speak. But if it is true, then it's a burden for you I can appreciate." He sneezed out his summer cold.

"Everybody's got their peculiar cross to bear. Right, Pard?"

I didn't answer since that seemed inarguable.

"Still, you might's well cozy up. We bedfellows in the same boat, as they say. Right, Pard?"

"You would think so to see us," I said, though I hoped that was patently untrue.

But the bars surrounding us were exactly the same to look at them, on all sides. But bars always look different from the outside than from the inside.

"And it ain't a White way to be, is it, Pard? Odds out in close quarters with a particular badass like myself."

He was about as puny as me but I nodded anyway.

He smiled, showing off his even, white teeth.

"See there, Pard? We understand one 'nother just about perfect. And for wise fellows like us only just takes that one word to the wise."

I stared at my fingernails, went to the basin and washed my hands in tepid water. There wasn't any soap and no towel and no toilet paper.

"What are you in for?" I inquired, sat back on the hard and narrow cot.

The man stretched, rubbed his crotch, at home, apparently, in jail.

"Disorder," he confessed.

"What kind of disorder?"

"Drunk and," he said. "What other kind is there?"

"Mental," I suggested.

He nodded agreeably, lifted two fingers.

"Really, Pard, it's two things. First off, I was fishing out at River Park this afternoon and Deputy Lloyd, he picks me up on drunken disorder."

He sneezed heartily, collected snot in his palm and wiped it on his blue jeans.

"And . . . ," he went on, stared at the ceiling as if he was wondering himself what the number-two thing was.

"It's a new oustanding on me for rape I just found out."

"Uh-huh," I said.

"That's my sister'n'law says I raped her."

"I see," I said.

"Which is a damned lie, Pard. Trust me on this one."

"Well," I said, "I don't know the whole story."

"Cain't say we ever do know that, Pard," he told me. "The whole story, what I mean."

He scratched in his thick, pomaded hair, pursed his lips, nodded to himself, spoke.

"Tidy Chicken, where we work at, is out on strike and me and my wife we was killing time over at my sister'n'law's house is the story."

He looked at me and I shrugged.

"You know her?"

"Who's that?" I asked.

"My wife, Hannah Lee."

"No."

"You know my sister'n'law then? Jucinda Lucille Harvey? Harvey's her married name. Her maiden name's Hayden. Not that she was ever no maiden."

I shook my head.

"Well, Pard, I just guess you ain't a sporting man then or you'd at least heard of her. Jucinda Lucille Harvey, second biggest whore in the Arkansas River Valley."

He frowned at me like I might be holding out on him somehow.

"She lives over at those trailer houses behind the Piggly Wiggly in Danielles, acrossed the Arkansas River. You know the ones?"

He seemed to want to connect me to the story someway. That seemed very important. I didn't feel connected, but maybe I was. Maybe everybody was connected, everybody everywhere responsible for everybody and everything.

I didn't particularly believe that. But it was a thought.

"I do know those trailer houses behind the Piggly Wiggly," I said.

"If you know them then you pro'bly might know Jucinda Harvey then," he posited hopefully.

I didn't know who he was. Didn't know who his people were. He did not seem to be anyone I wanted to know. And I was not particularly interested in gaining new friends.

Still it can pay to be cordial.

"I just might," I allowed.

"All right then," he said. "Then you know it's just a whorestown over there, all it is. 'Bout as bad as Doker. Might's well paint the whole trailer park red and put up a price sign."

"Uh-huh," I said.

"So you know how it is," he told me.

I wasn't sure I wanted to know how it was, was not certain at all that I wanted to even talk to this jailbird, if that's what he was. But there is something magnetic about ignorant degenerates and trashy whores, and time passes slowly in jail, as they say. And the unregenerate serve as scapegoats some way maybe, balance the scales of humanity perhaps. We're all crooked, but some of us are stupid too, some of us get caught; and those of us who aren't stupid and don't get caught feel better that those of us who are and do are there, here, everywhere serving as a reminder that it could be worse for us, that we could be worse.

And it didn't appear I was going anywhere soon. So I nodded.

"So me and my wife, Hannah Lee, we was over there in that trailer park behind the Piggly Wiggly last afternoon, killing time and my sister'n'law, who holds liquor like a fishnet, got fucked up was what happened and her husband, man name of T. Bo Harvey, works at the Exxon station over in Doker in your part of the woods. Volunteer fireman sometimes . . . You know T. Bo?"

I shook my head.

"Well, he's gone over there to Doker all the time," my neighbor said thoughtfully, like that could explain it, the whole mess he was in.

"I think he gets his over there too. What I hear from Jucinda Lucille, T. Bo he doesn't get it at home from her."

I nodded, kneaded my eyeballs with my knuckles, inhaled, exhaled.

"So Jucinda Lucille she knows me and my old lady, her own sister, hadn't been doing it of late 'cause of Hannah Lee's got a yeast infection. So she's working up to me all night long. You know how it is. I got a fearsome big dick. Her husband's gone off. Finally I had enough of that shit, so I told her if she wanted it so bad I'd surely give it to her. What else could a man do?"

He stared at me like I might not understand his reasoning, though I could, totally.

"Uh-huh," I said.

"Shit's truth, Pard," he claimed, sneezed. "Of course just looking at you I might think women were not your thing, no offense, so I couldn't say for you. But for me, Pard, it's the sporting life morning, noon and night, whenever, wherever. So I poked ol' Jucinda right up her ass in the bathroom of her double-wide."

"Where was your wife at this time?"

He thought about this.

"My wife was just passed out in the living room."

"Uh-huh," I said.

"It's Gospel, Pard."

He raised the Boy Scout fingers, sneezed and wiped his nose on his pledging hand.

"Jucinda Lucille asked for it outright, as you heard me tell for yourself. What's did me in though, was coming in her porthole. Jucinda Lucille hates that and I knew she hated it and I went on and did it just the same."

He nodded at me like I'd understand that.

"And, Pard, that's why she called the Law on my dumb-ass self."

He acted like Life was a very simple proposition but for the details and his forgetfulness of them.

"I see," I said.

He sighed sincerely.

"I hope Sammy the Man don't let you out, Pard," he told me. "No offense, but I'm in here awhile and I hate to lose a winner like you. Good listener hard to find in this shithole. Mostly just niggers. Not that I got anything against niggers themselves, but they just not like us, Pard. And like to like, I say."

I wasn't sure I appreciated the comparison.

I wasn't entirely sure that I could disagree with it though.

My jail cell neighbor looked me up and then down.

"You live out at Rushing, don't you, Pard?"

He said that like he knew it for a fact.

It did not seem wise to confirm to the man where I lived.

"I think you do," my jail mate said. "I think you that rich fella my pardner Jake Wells told me about. The one that bought the Old Duncan spread a little while back. That you, Pard? You that crazy Texas fella Jake tells me about that throws rocks at his cows and his kids? Likes to go down to Hot Springs?"

I shrugged like I didn't know who I was.

"Well, them kids a' Jake's—Isaac and Neutron, if you can believe those dumb-ass names—are little green shits that need to get stomped on, Pard, if I do say so."

I didn't say anything, because this too was inarguable.

My jail neighbor coughed and spit on the floor on his side of the bars.

"You know your buddy Sammy Baxter's got a place out yonder too."

"The sheriff does?" I asked.

"Yup. That place the other side of The Little Piney, the spread that's got the badass fence 'roundabout it."

"Really?" I said.

"Sworn truth, Pard. Why would I lie 'bout a thing like that of all things?"

I didn't know the answer to that question and I must have looked a wee bit surprised since my new jailhouse buddy continued with his data dump.

"Sammy was born and raised out over there, lived there every day until he run off to join the Marines Corp. His own momma was a schoolteach over at Doker High. Very sweet woman. Loved cats. And his daddy used to raise up apples. Me and Jake just about lived off them apples when we was kids."

"What happened to Baxter's folks?"

"His momma died a cancer while back. His daddy went crazed as a coot short while after that fact. Old man still stays out over in there what I hear. Not in the house, but outside. Won't sleep inside. What that fence is all about— to keep the old loon penned up."

"You're serious?"

"As a heart attack. Tried to put old man Baxter in a crazy house over in Fort Smith, but he hurt some people and broke out. I guess Sam figures his daddy, he's 'bout's well off out there in the woods as in town."

I wondered about that.

The locks on the door to our cell block clicked. It wasn't a loud sound, but I was keen to hear it. I stood up as a fat deputy walked our way.

"Mr. Reynolds," he called out. "Pack your bags, Sir. Freedom train's acoming your way."

The deputy opened my cell, stepped aside to let me pass by into the aisle, locked the gate shut again, looked at my ex-neighbor.

"You been yapping all this time, Ricky Dale?"

"Just being neighborly, Deputy Lloyd," said Ricky Dale to the jailer. To me he said, "I'll come visit you at Rushing when I get out, Pard."

"Long's you're going to be in the can this time, Ricky Dale, he probably won't even be living out there after all that time. Will you, Mr. Reynolds?"

I shrugged.

"Or might be too old by then to remember you, Ricky Dale," the deputy added.

"See you," Ricky Dale said to me anyway. "Pard."

"Stay out of trouble," I said.

I sort of expected somebody to be there, one of my law-yers, a judge, the sheriff, somebody, anybody with an explanation.

But there was nobody except Deputy Lloyd beside me. He locked the block down, stepped behind the booking desk and started searching under the counter.

"You got some valuables here, Sir?" he asked me.

I pressed a hand against my chest. The wedding band, the gold ring on the chain around my neck, the property of the dead man, was gone. My own wedding ring was still on my finger. My wallet and car keys, I thought, were in the pickup.

"I don't know," I said.

The deputy looked under the counter again.

"I don't see a thing, Sir."

He pushed a form at me, held out a pen, jerked his head at the hallway that led to the sidewalk.

"Sign this release form then, Sir, and you can go on."

"What if I don't sign?"

"Everybody always signs, Sir. You'll surely want to sign too."

I signed.

"That's it?" I asked.

"Far's I'm concerned," the deputy said. "Sheriff called in and said to drop the trespass charge against Randall Reynolds and let him out. Sheriff Baxter had you crimi-nal trespassing dead to rights as I heard it. He let you loose on that. You got some complaint, Sir?"

I guessed I didn't. My head was sore and I was hungry, filthy and tired, but free and really none the worse for wear after a few hours in jail.

At my age I never felt too good anyway.

"You want me to call you a taxicab, Sir?"

"I guess I'll just walk up to the Holiday Inn and get some dinner."

I had a running tab at the Inn, so didn't need my wallet for that.

"Sorry about you missing lunch, Sir, but you was sleeping so sound I couldn't see waking you up for jailhouse grub. Downtime pass quicker when you're out of it."

I nodded.

"So, I'm to understand I got arrested and jailed for trespassing on Sheriff Baxter's property?"

"Criminal trespass, yes Sir. And if that doesn't suit you, Sheriff said he could press charges for breaking and entering besides and that might suit you."

I rubbed the bump on the back of my head.

"I guess I'll pass on that," I said and moved toward the door. "Good-bye, Officer. I hope I won't be seeing you again under these same circumstances."

"It'd be in your best interests, Sir," the sheriff's deputy replied. "We'll wait and see."

I stopped at the door.

"You know anything about a man found dead in The Little Piney this afternoon?"

Deputy Lloyd wrinkled his forehead, frowned for a while and finally nodded, as if he had just made a judgment call.

I wondered if he was supposed to be telling or not telling.

"Sorry business, Sir. Drug-related, Sheriff speculates."

"Who was it?"

"Used to be a local fellow."

"You know his name?"

"Waiting for Dr. Williams to do the autopsy and next-of-kin notifying, so I couldn't say, Sir," he told me. "You know something about it?"

I shook my head.

The deputy nodded, advised.

"That's good, Sir. And if I was you, I wouldn't say nothing to nobody about nothing for a while. A good little while. Maybe you could even take a trip, Sir. I understand you are partial to Hot Springs."

"Does that come from Sheriff Baxter?"

"You said that, Sir, not me."

He settled into a chair, closed his eyes.

"Let a word to the wise be sufficient, Sir."

I figured that as sound advice.

But it didn't exactly sit well all the same.

CHAPTER 7

The walk to the Holiday Inn was through downtown Bertrandville where most of the storefronts were boarded up, telling the regular story of small-town America, of family-owned and -operated establishments forced out of business by Wholesale Clubs and Supercenters ensconced on low-rent property in the suburbs, or into relocation at the Valley Mall where the sidewalks were inside and air-conditioned and the parking free and plentiful.

I couldn't care less.

The downtown desolation didn't bother me in general and neither did the B'ville Mall specifically as I didn't shop much and when I did I bought sensible shoes through the mail, shoes that never seemed to fit but lasted a long time. So nobody was making much money off me anyhow.

It was about a mile and a half to the Holiday Inn.

My heel blister flared up again along the way. My sensible mail-order shoes had failed me yet again.

❧

It was midafternoon so the Crow's Nest was mostly empty, but for Professor Ford at the bar and a couple of regular businessmen still lingering over a very late liquid lunch or an early liquid supper. One of them bumped into me as I made my way toward the bar.

"Hello there, Fella, my name's Hunter B. Briggs and I been with Tidy Chicken Industries for over three years and increased sales over four percent in my region in those three plus years I been with them which is over one percent per year and I don't even have a business degree from college, Fella."

"That's nice for you, Mr. Briggs."

I had heard this exact same spiel from Hunter B. Briggs a dozen times.

"Fella, because it's you, I will tell you my secret," Hunter B. Briggs offered.

I didn't encourage him. Because I knew enough secrets.

"Employ your predatory instincts, Fella. That's the real secret to business life," he confided. "Take advantage when advantage is there. Kick 'em when they're down and then eat 'em right up. It pure piddly works, Fella. Believe me on this one."

"That's good news to me, Mr. Briggs."

"I don't tell everybody, Fella."

"I guess I'll just mosey over to the bar now and jot that down, Mr. Briggs," I said.

"Pred-a-tory," he whispered. "Hunter B. Briggs told you first, Fella."

"I appreciate you, Mr. Briggs."

Having been reared in a peculiar, financially conservative environment, by a mother whose greatest fiscal indulgences were ankle-length denim housedresses and Bibles and a father who considered alcohol the only worthwhile expenditure to make on recreation, there were not a lot of luxuries I could allow myself without a mean guilt nagging me.

Being rich, in other words, is not the pleasure to someone like me that it is to a regular hedonist.

I bought sensible but pricey mail-order shoes (which nonetheless consistently failed to meet my expectations for comfort). I ate my breakfast at a café almost every day (even though Miss Ollie's cooking at EAT left much to be desired on the cuisine level, on the calorie level it was very cost effective). I could afford to pay Tammy Fay's exorbitant rates for automobile repairs (even though these were ridiculously inexpert automotive repairs).

I also had a running tab at the Holiday Inn and Convention Center in Bertrandville, prepaid enough every month to cover my bar and restaurant bills and room rent for when I was too drunk to drive home or came to town to use the swimming pool or watch TV with the Crow's Nest contingent.

As a Privileged Regular I also got to receive telephone messages at the bar. There were standard rates for this service—so much to say you were there at the bar, so much more to say you weren't there at the bar, so much more even than that to pass on a fabrication about where you were.

I had never had to avail myself of any of these telephone services.

But, like the spider in my mailbox, I had hopes.

❧

"Hey you, Mr. Jailbird."

"Hey you, Ladoris," I replied to the day-shift bartender, a coal-black woman with shoulder-length hair plaited and segmented by colored wooden beads.

"You don't look so good."

When she shook her head at me her hair rattled.

"Thanks for noticing, Ladoris."

None of the regulars but Professor Ford, three sheets to the wind already, were at the bar.

I leaned over my fellow poet's tweedy shoulder and read what he had written on a cocktail napkin.

What I know of bears and their habits
Informs my morning stroll.
In the evening there are snakes on the road.

"Sounds like a pretty ominous world," I suggested.

Ford crumpled up the napkin verse and tossed it to Ladoris, who dunked it into the trash can. He was always very competitive about his napkin poems and I hoped to construct one that would challenge that one.

"Seems of late it might have been so for you," Dr. Ford said. "Ominous and unpredictable for yourself, Laureate."

This moniker was a needle from the good professor who had once qualified for a National Book Award. Not recognizing who he was when we had first met many months before I had made the mistake of mentioning (just in passing, mind) that I had once received an EggCrate Award for a chapbook of poems I had more or less self-published. And that was the beginning of our civil unpleasantness.

I sat down on my regular barstool two removed from the professor.

The air in the Nest was thick with lingering cigar smoke, hairspray and cologne. Outside the plate-glass windows, poolside, a bevy of chunky teenaged girls shrieked as they practiced a complicated maneuver.

Cheerleaders.

"Our notable honoree here obviously needs a drink, Ladoris dear," Ford said. "A heady Merlot, would be, I believe, most suitable," he decided for me.

It was early but I nodded.

"Sorry to hear of your arrest, Laureate," said Ford. "I know it is a burdensome task to labor under the freighted, dark cloud of criminal suspicion."

Ford had been drummed out of the local university for leveraging sex from students, had lost his tenure, been forced into early retirement and almost convicted of something egregious.

"Apparently I got arrested," I said. "But then released without charge."

"A pity, Laureate. But, as well, your story represents a version of classic tragedy, really. A dumbed-down version, to be certain, but a tragedy in the classical sense nonetheless. I think you understand me, as you are versed in the Classics."

I wasn't, particularly, but I nodded.

"How did you hear about my arrest, Professor?"

Ford partook of an especially long draught of his Merlot, then burped a very liquid burp.

"Our mutual acquaintance, Dr. Doc Williams, indulged us his company for lunch. He was our font of information. He was our oracle, Laureate. You understand me when I speak, don't you? You do, of course. You were a Greek at some time. Scion of Hippocrates."

"Doc is," I clarified. "A scion of Hippocrates."

I myself was a scion of simple upper-middle-class success or perhaps some old Stoics.

Ford looked at me as if I had only just arrived and had perhaps taken the wrong seat. He was obviously more drunk than usual that day.

"And what then has occurred to you lately, Laureate? You have won another grand prize, I take it?"

"Sheriff Baxter arrested me for trespassing," I explained again. "Criminal trespassing. But then he dropped the charges."

"Overjoyed to hear of it, Laureate. Overjoyed to hear that you have won your freedom . . ." He paused to gather some steam. "That you are free. Free to run, to win prizes more galore. To grasp Life by the throat and give it a good throttling."

Ford lifted a shaky hand toward the dropped ceiling.

"The darkest of dark clouds have parted for you. And you, my noble Laureate, are free to run now into the light."

"You think so, Professor," I said.

I leaned down and felt the blister just inside the back rim of my left loafer.

"Oh surely, my Laureate. It's the silver lining saga. It's all written in the book. Can't you see it there?"

He aimed an oscillating finger at a Styrofoam ceiling tile.

"A silver lining on an ominous, ebony cloud. And you, Laureate of Laureates, running free under that bright silver lining. It is a happy ending. A happy, happy ending to a sad, classically tragic tale. A happy ending that warms the cockles. And I do so look forward to a story with a happy ending that I must thank you, my friendly poetic rival. Thank you for this story with this happy ending. Thank you."

Ford was even "drunker than usual" than usual.

"Sure, Professor," I said.

I reached over the bar top for a pen and a coaster and wrote a short poem myself:

I like the female
Spider who eats her stale mate
And then shits pure silk

I slid the coaster in front of the poetry professor. He read what was written around "Coors Light," then shook his hoary head dismissively. Still he was gracious.

"Thank you for that, Poet Laureate. Whatever it was supposed to be. A haiku I can only imagine."

Ford began to scribble again another napkin poem and I was tempted to join him in this strange fray, to take up pen in this heated exchange of signs and symbols, and enter again this semiotic battle. But I was too tired to participate further.

When he saw me slide my coaster and pen into the bar trough he took this as capitulation and put his own Montblanc away, sliding his extravagant pen into his unnecessary tweed jacket.

"What do you know about Sheriff Sam Baxter, Professor?"

"High Sheriff is a reasonable man," Ford replied thoughtfully a longish moment later. "As are they all. All reasonable men."

"Is he?" I asked, pressing the point. "Reasonable?"

"High Sheriff is a reasonable man if you precisely suit his purposes, Laureate," Ford allowed. "But not many do precisely suit his purposes."

"I'm just glad to be out of jail."

"And I am glad for you, Laureate. But should the need arise again I am overly familiar with an excellent local investigator type. A student of mine from the old days. Fine private eye and impersonator and negotiator and not too shabby a performer in bed. Not much to look at, if you understand me, Laureate, but he has got a fearsome big dick. And he works sometimes for the sheriff's department, as a snitch as they say, so he knows, as they say, the ropes."

Ford eyeballed me.

"Thanks, Professor," I said. "But I have some lawyers in Texas and elsewhere on retainer already. And I don't think I need a snitch in local law enforcement or a private eye."

"Just a word to the wise, Laureate. If ever you need a local liaison. This fellow is well acquainted, as they say, with the ropes. You would not think it to look at this boy, but he knows all the law and all the lawmen." Ford took a sip of his merlot. "Local matters can be prickly at times, especially when those matters touch on we Poetic Types, my Laureate. Prickly and peculiar about we inverted 'poets' can they be in these unenlightened parts."

"I appreciate the advice, Professor."

"Which is, I would imagine, preferable to being 'depreciated' I assume?" He asked this rhetorically, so I did not respond.

The poet tossed a twenty on the bar and wobbled away without farewelling.

Ladoris snatched the cash, set a shot of bourbon and a draft beer, my regular order (not Merlot), in front of me.

I threw Jim Beam to the back of my throat, chased him home with Adolf Coors.

Ladoris turned up the volume on the house radio when she heard her favorite Prince start explaining what happens when doves cry.

❧

So, Deputy Lloyd had not divulged any news to me about the fact of the corpse in the creek except that the dead man was a "Local" of one sort or another. But "Local" could cover some ground. Local for Malcolm was only the several miles from The Little Piney to Goody's Grocery Store in Doker. Local for most Locals meant from Doker or Bertrandville, which were "dry" towns that did not sell beer, wine or liquor, only as far as anyplace going any direction that was "wet" and did sell beer, wine or liquor. For Ladoris North Little Rock remained local for her since she had just landed in Bertrandville for college and stayed for graduate school. There were not a lot of black people in Bertrandville and Ladoris did not, frankly, have much interest in white people, local or otherwise.

"You seen Smarty Bell, Ladoris?" I asked the bartender.

"Out back in the Dumpster taking care of his moonshine delivery. He'll be in shortly." She glanced at me. "You okay, Hon? You don't look so good."

I showed her the lump on the back of my head.

She made a sympathetic noise but then went to the far end of the bar and started washing wine stems.

Smarty Bell shoved through the service entrance after a while, with a wooden apple crate full of mason jars full of clear corn liquor.

"Welcome back to the free world, Buddy."

Smarty Bell stowed the moonshine in a trash can, then gave my sore shoulder a squeeze.

"I told you not to mess with Baxter, Bud."

I nodded.

"I'll call you in a steak," he said, picked up the house phone. "Medium rare?" he asked.

I nodded, though I always ordered my steak well done.

Smarty Bell relayed the order to the kitchen, recradled the phone. It rang immediately. Smarty Bell picked up, grunted a couple of times, hung up.

"That was Doc Williams, Bud. Looking for you. I told

him you'd be here for a while, so he can give you a ride back to Doker."

"Okay, Smarty Bell."

I went to the restroom and washed my face and neck, washed my hands for a while, returned to my barstool and ate my meal when it arrived, chewed every bite twenty times.

Smarty Bell kept my beer mug filled, but apart from inquiring that once about my health he didn't speak to me much, went about his regular business, as per usual.

Outside the cheerleaders practiced indefatigably.

I paid strict attention to them as long as possible.

Then I lay my head on the bar and closed my eyes.

"Bob."

Doc was beside me. The TV was on. The jukebox was on too. The bar was beginning to fill up with Party Locals. The cheerleaders were gone from the poolside, seemed to have moved inside and morphed into their own big-haired mothers, smoking skinny cigarettes and drinking thick, colorful drinks.

Smarty Bell put a cup of coffee in front of the doctor.

"Are you ready to amble on back home, Bob?" Dr. Doc asked me. "You about made a day of it, seems to me."

"Somebody made a day of it," I said.

I rubbed my eyes, trying to wake up.

"They treat you all right in County?" Doc asked me.

"I just slept mostly," I admitted.

"Ladoris said something about a lump on your head."

I showed off my injury.

"Looks like a lawsuit," Smarty Bell said.

But then everything was pretty much a lawsuit for

Smarty Bell, who always had several litigations ongoing. He sued his vendors so often he sometimes could not even get a bottle of beer and bag of chips delivered for a week. He sued his taxidermist for making his bigmouth bass look too small and for stealing points from the racks of his trophyized deer. He sued his ex-wives because they sued him. He had sued Professor Ford for, quote, "being a faggot in my business establishment and declining my profits." He had not sued me yet, but only because I was still constantly apologizing to him for having once called him a "shrimphead."

"I don't think Bob was considering suing Poe County, Smarty Bell," the doctor said, as if he was quite sure about this. "Were you, Bob?"

"I'm still not sure what even happened," I said. "But no, I hadn't thought of suing anybody. I guess I could though."

"I'd sue his ass off," said Smarty Bell. "But it wouldn't be wise for a fella like you, Bud." The barkeep advised me, "Baxter could make hell for a guy like you. Alls he's got to do is plant a gram of coke in your house or your truck and bag you like a crippled quail on crutches. Happens all the time to outsiders like you when they pass through here." When he pointed at my face I thought he was going to call me a little foreign shrimphead as he sometimes did, but he just repeated himself in a friendly warning way. "Happens all the time, Buddy."

"Sam wouldn't do that, Smarty," Doc said quietly. "The sheriff does not plant evidence and fabricate false charges. He's an officer of the Law."

"And I'm the Pope's boyfriend just nobody's talking about it," Smarty Bell said. "Local corruption is the elephant in the room."

"That's uncalled for, Smarty," Doc said.

"May be," admitted Smarty Bell. "But I warned this little shrimphead since he was foreign he should not consider being a smart-ass with Baxter," the barkeep reminded me. "And it seems like my little buddy here *did* consider it and so . . ." Smarty popped his bar towel like a whip to accentuate his point.

"I told you he was always loaded for bear, Bud. I told you so."

"I know," I said.

"I know you know, Bud. But still and all, you went on and acted like your regular smart-ass self," judged Smarty Bell. "And you see exactly where it got you. Just like when you called me a shrimphead. You see how that worked out. Not to your advantage."

"I apologize for calling you a 'shrimphead', Smarty Bell. I meant to say 'shrimpdick' but it came out wrong."

Smarty Bell snapped the bar rag right next to my ear. I flinched at the *POP!*

"And you see what happened when you took that smart mouth of yours over to play at the sheriff's house."

"I got incarcerated," I said.

But not killed.

"Damned straight. And now you're talking about suing . . ."

"Bob is not talking 'bout suing anybody, Smarty Bell," Doc interrupted. "Quit putting your ideas into his head. Bob is a sensible person. As is the sheriff. This is all just a minor misunderstanding that will blow over," the doctor insisted. "Blow over very shortly and then we can all return to normal."

"Whatever that is around here," Ladoris said from the far end of the bar, sotto voce.

I counted to ten and then back to one, inhaled, exhaled ten deep breaths.

Doc took a long drink of coffee, wiped his mouth with a bloody handkerchief.

"Let most wise counsel prevail when affairs of state are in unrest, gentlemen," declared the doctor. "Most Wise Counsel being me. Bob is not suing the Poe County Sheriff's Department. I am taking him home."

"Fine," I said, and stood. "See you, Smarty Bell."

"See you around the well, Bud."

Doc and I walked out of the Crow's Nest.

Outside in a dusky sky a pair of stars were faintly appealing.

CHAPTER 8

In his capacity as Poe County medical examiner Dr. Doc drove an olive-green station wagon with GOVERNMENT USE ONLY plates. The vehicle was much abused, scraped and buckled. The smell of corpses hauled to the morgue made my nostril hairs curl.

Doc established himself on the driver's side, extracted a can of disinfectant from under his seat, blasted a spray over our shoulders.

"Sorry for the scent, Bob. Death does stink, but it has its purposes," Doc said. "Like 'most everything else."

By the time we were over the bridge spanning the Interstate the scent of his pipe tobacco overwhelmed the scent of collected dead bodies. Doc turned on the radio and Hank Williams sounded so lonesome.

The outskirts of Bertrandville was trailer parks and low-tech industry that looked like giant aluminum shoeboxes and giant bricks dropped randomly in cow pastures without a thought to architecture or urban planning. We passed the Pancake House and the Waffle House, Wonder Burger, Shoney's, Scottish Inn, Motel 6, RW King's Tire Palace.

"As Sam reported the incident to me, Bob, you were trespassing—" Doc started.

"Stop the car, Doc," I interrupted. "Pull over, please."

I guess I looked queasy because Doc immediately braked in the parking lot of RW King's Tire Palace.

I hopped out of the station wagon, backtracked a hundred yards to the Motel 6, walked through the parking lot slowly, went into the office.

"May I help you, Sir?"

I looked over my shoulder.

"I'm with the Poe County Medical Examiner," I said, truthfully enough. "I want to know who owns that maroon Oldsmobile Cutlass sedan parked out behind the dumpster. It's got big, whippy antennas on it, Arkansas license plate number BCK FVR."

The desk clerk stared at me. I blinked.

"Don't I need to see some . . . some ID, maybe? Officer?"

"I'm afraid I don't have my ID, young man."

Doc stepped into the office.

"Bob? Are you checking into a motel?" the doctor asked. "I was quite certain that I was taking you home."

"Dr. Williams, have you got your Medical Examiner Identification Card with you?"

"I don't believe I ever had one, Bob," said the local ME. "Everybody just knows me."

I shrugged at the desk clerk, who seemed satisfied by this level of tertiary and suspect identification, so he took the easy route and copied information off a registration slip and handed me a sticky note.

"When did you last see this fellow, Leo King, young man?" I asked. "The man who owns the Olds Cutlass?"

"He prepaid for a week on last Sunday, Officer, but I haven't seen him since then at all. I hadn't even seen his car in a while. Didn't have any idea it was parked out there 'til ya'll pointed it out me."

"Bob," Doc said. "I think we should be going now."

I nodded briskly at the desk clerk.

"We thank you for your cooperation, young man."

"Yessir, Officer."

Doc led me by the elbow outside. I tucked the note into my T-shirt pocket, got back into the meat wagon.

Doc steered us onto the highway without checking for traffic.

"Bob, what was all that about?"

"Business," I said.

Bob Reynolds business.

❦

We rode toward Doker in silence. Doc was probably thinking. I counted thirteen speed limit signs, all of which the doctor ignored.

There was raised-up ground around us that could have been big hills or small mountains, depending on your perspective. I had come to the area from the flat Gulf Shore so I supposed the mounds were the fractured last bits of the Boston Mountains, near cousins to the Ozarks. This isolated, extruded ridge Locals called the Grays, a name earned because, drenched in westering light, the piles of granite resembled a line of blood-splattered Confederate kepi caps with bayonets raised among them here and there in feeble defense against the setting sun.

I didn't see this scene from what Locals still persisted in calling The War myself, but a lot of what the natives saw escaped my perception.

The music on the car radio was country western, but not country and not western.

❦

"It might serve our collective purposes better if you just start the story from the beginning, Bob," Doc instructed as he slowed the speeding wagon only slightly at the Doker city limits sign.

How could anyone ever say where the beginning of anything was?

And I wasn't sure what "collective purpose" the good doctor and I might have in common.

I wasn't even sure what my individual purpose was.

I had a feeling, though, that I had gone about as far toward it as I was willing to go. That to go farther was to go too far. That the story might soon tell of my exit.

"Who were you autopsying today, Doc?"

He raised his shaggy white eyebrows, pursed his lips, shook his head, parked on Main Street.

"I have been instructed not to say, Bob."

"Someone you knew?"

"I know everybody, Bob."

He frowned as if that knowledge was disagreeable. He motioned toward his office.

"I want to give you a quick checkup, Bob," Doc said. "Gratis."

"Okay, Doc."

I was not one to turn down free medical attention.

Downtown Doker was pretty much deserted. A three-legged dog wandered the sidewalk in front of the closed-down First National Bank building.

I whistled a call.

The damaged old bluetick barked once sharply, sniffed the hot, dry air, then barked steadily in my direction.

"Come 'ere, Stank," I called Tammy Fay's dog.

The bitch hound hobbled to me and nuzzled my leg. I scratched her ass, the rubbed-raw spot near the base of her tail, as Doc unlocked his storefront.

"Dog likes you, Bob."

I didn't put much weight on canine opinion. Stank saw

me almost every morning, knew me and I usually gave her a treat to stop her barking, so she liked me and that's the way it goes with a dog's affections more often than not.

A lot of good dogs like bad people. As a lot of bad dogs like good people.

"Let's us step into the office a minute before we run you to your house," Doc said. "I'll give that sore head of yours a couple of stitches. We can talk inside."

Fluorescent bulbs buzzed and bathed the waiting area in unnaturally white light. Outside Stank barked and barked.

"It's Nurse's day off, Bob, so give me a minute to set up."

Doc went off behind frosted glass. It sounded like he uncradled a telephone, murmured. I picked up a year-old *National Geographic* with a gorilla on the cover, tossed the magazine back on a plastic couch and studied the photographs that covered one wall of Doc's office.

His dead wife was there prominently—as a new bride with a stiff new Doc in a couple of shots; alone, variously aged, unposed in others; hugging unrelated children in a few; older, shoulder to shoulder with another woman in one, she smiling, the other not. Doc's wife had a very winning smile that looked natural, but apart from that she was not attractive.

"Melissa," Doc said.

He had come up behind me unnoticed.

"We couldn't have kids of our own, so she got into the habit of appropriating the dispossessed."

I guess I looked like I was not following his train of thought, because he added some explanation.

"She started this camp for kids. She wanted to call it Camp of Hope, but I thought that was . . . well, a little too ambitious, I guess. So we wrangled about it until we arrived at a compromise, as we usually did."

"What was the place called, Doc?"

"Camp Osage."

It seemed a long way from Camp of Hope to Camp Osage, so I gathered this "compromise" was like most of the compromises I'd encountered, unilateral. Doc seemed to be the sort to make "suggestions" that carried the same force as "orders."

"I guess you still miss her, Doc?"

"There was only one of her in existence, Bob," he said, sort of avoiding the simple answer I thought he would give. "Can't help but miss an extinguished species, can you?"

I pondered his answer for a moment, wondering about it, poetic as it sounded.

"Ever think about remarrying?"

"At my age, Bob, no point in trying, since you can't usually get what you want anyway. You of all people should understand that."

I stared at the wall, not sure how to take that.

I had never paid much attention to the doctor's Wall of Fame, the diplomas there and the photographs. Several drew my attention though now, seemed suddenly pertinent.

I leaned over the plastic sofa and touched the glass protecting a faded picture of a trio of crew-cutted soldiers in fatigues, two of whom looked familiar—one looked like a version of the dead man, seen recently in The Little Piney, perhaps Buck's father. The other, redressed in civilian garb and forty years older now stood right behind me, Doc Williams.

"That was Dick King," Doc informed me. "We shipped to Korea at the same time and never got separated. His people were from Arkadelphia and I got him to move to Bertrandville after our duties were done. My daddy loaned him the money to start up his first tire store. We were quite the whippersnappers back then."

"Dick have a son?" I asked.

"Leonard," Doc said, real soft. "Called him Buck. Looked just like his daddy. Spitting image. Come on back to the exam room now, Bob."

I didn't move.

"You said, 'looked,' Doc. Buck 'looked' just like his daddy. Past tense."

Doc didn't say anything. I kept focused on the wall.

"You figure the fellow in The Little Piney was Leonard 'Buck' King, your Korea buddy's son?"

The corpse I had found in the creek matched in his looks the man in the photo near exactly—my dead man had to have been the son of Doc's old friend from Korea.

Doc answered me with silence.

"Who's the other fellow in Korea with you and Mr. King, Doc?"

Doc sighed and his breath was musty and moist on the back of my neck.

"That's me and Dick King, Buck's daddy . . . ," Doc told me. "And Samuel Baxter Senior."

Beside the snapshot of the soldiers was a teenaged football player in Doker Buccaneers red and black, padded, but still shortish, lean and mean as a greased M16. A young Sheriff Sam Baxter. Next to that sports shot a formal portrait of a Marine. Again Sheriff Sam Baxter.

"Samuel Baxter Senior, your old buddy, is the sheriff's daddy?"

"Yes, Bob. That's the sheriff's mother, Frances, there with my wife, Melissa. Frances had just been diagnosed with lung cancer. Never smoked a cigarette in her life, but Samuel smoked like a chimney. Melissa and Frances were both passed within two years. Both cancer."

Doc walked behind the frosted glass, made a racket with metal medical paraphernalia.

I examined the rest of Doc's wall, mostly baby pictures,

saw Malcolm. I didn't see much else to pique my interest, save for one oldish group photo of a mixed bunch of people, ranging from little kids to adults.

Spanning the length of the wide-angle shot was a severely homemade banner that identified the gang as tribesmen of CAMP OSAGE—1970.

Centered in the shot was an obviously beleaguered Mrs. Melissa Williams. On one side of her was a kid I recognized as the brain-damaged son of Miss Ollie Ames, Warnell Ames. On the other side of the camp administrator was a young version of Sheriff Sam Baxter, somewhere around his midtwenties probably, crew-cutted, GI-dressed, home from the Corps. A pale, skinny white kid was Malcolm's daddy maybe, Joe Pickens Junior. Anchoring one end of the banner was Dr. Doc Williams, even then looking like an old man.

The other end of the banner was upheld by a willowy, white blond–headed girl, just in her teens or maybe even a tall ten- or twelve-year-old—though Tammy Fay looked old in the eyes already. Those deep-set eyes as seen in the photo were cast over her shoulder at the thick-necked man in a GI-green T-shirt looming over her, who was a young grown man, roughly handsome, though, with a meaty face under a severe high and tight crew cut. But this young jarhead was not Sam Baxter—this was Leonard "Buck" King.

Buck's arm was snaked around the tall girl's waist.

Photographic film interprets faces in its own peculiar way. So I couldn't tell if Tammy Fay was happy to have the man's arm around her or if she was pissed. In my experience she was usually pissed at the world but liked the attention it provided her.

The big GI giving her the attention in the old photo seemed matured well beyond high school, also in his midtwenties at least. I did the math in my head. It was fourteen years since this group photo from Camp Osage—1970, so Buck would be around forty years old now to Tammy Fay's midtwenties. Buck had been a big man in the real world. But in the photo hanging on the doctor's wall, Buck was covered by the thumb I pressed over him.

The tattoo on his forearm was just a black smear with wings.

I guessed the worded inscription on Buck King's flesh was *Semper Fidelis.*

"You might want to clench your jaw right about now, Bob," my physician advised.

I felt the air cold on the shaved circle at the base of my skull. Swabbed-on alcohol stung tears into my eyes.

"You sure I need stitches, Doc?" I asked, shifted on the examination table. The fresh white paper rustled under my ass.

"Who's the medical expert here, Bob?"

"I'm sure a lot of your patients have asked that same question, Doc."

The curved needle slipped into my head, the string pulled through my scalp.

"I take that back," I said, ripped the table paper.

"Sorry I couldn't locate the deadening accoutrements, Bob. I'm at a loss without Nurse, you know."

The needle, the string ran their course again, the second naturally following the first. My toes curled in my walking shoes.

"You said, two, Doc. Just two stitches."

"Several, I said, Bob. And you know I'm an old-fashioned doc, always erring on the side of conservative policy. Better to overdo some things than underdo them. You wouldn't want those fine brains of yours spilling out in your sleep, would you, Bob?"

The needle went in, the needle went out. The cold steel was not getting any warmer.

"That's it," I declared, started to get up.

Doc pressed me back onto the table.

He was surprisingly strong for an old man.

"You ever hear the one about the duck at the bar, Bob?"

"I told you that one."

"Just thinking of what Voltaire said about physicians."

I felt a tug at the base of my skull.

"That the art of medicine consists mainly of amusing the patient while God effects the cure."

"I don't know about god," I said, "but you need to work on your jokes, Doc."

Doc tied off the stitches, severed the string between us. I stood and felt the bristling on the back of my head, below my bald spot.

"You tell that buddy of yours, Sam Baxter, the fellow that sapped me to unconsciousness, that if I'd needed one more stitch on the back of my head I would have sued."

Doc straightened up his paraphernalia.

"I doubt that was a wound from a leather sap, Bob."

"Meaning?"

The Poe County Medical Examiner stripped off the old white paper and rolled a fresh sheet out, pulled it tight and clipped it to the sides of the table.

"The wound on your head is not consistent with the description of a wound suffered from a policeman's leather sap."

I raised my eyebrows.

"The skin was broken. In a jagged fashion. Not serious, but inconsistent with the profile of a sap wound. I cleaned out some rock dust and fragments as well."

"A rock?"

"You could have fallen. Sam says you did."

"What exactly is the sheriff's version, Doc? I know you're tight with Baxter. I guess you've known him since he was a baby."

"I delivered Sam," Doc said. "In that house I helped his daddy build, the one across The Little Piney. Helped Samuel plant his apple trees and press his first batch of cider. Melissa introduced him to Frances Roberts."

Doc switched off the examining room lights, held back the frosted glass door for me. I passed out of that room and into the waiting area, looked again at the doctor's Wall of Fame, at the cast of Locals, the babies delivered, the football hero High Sheriff, his momma, his daddy, the doctor's dead wife, the doctor's diplomas, Tammy Fay as a child, the dead man in The Little Piney with a tattooed forearm around her waist, Miss Ollie Ames's hulking son Warnell.

"It's right here, isn't it, Doc?" I asked. "The story is right here."

"It's really a local matter, Bob."

"And the sheriff's version of today's events?" I repeated my earlier query.

"Sam had you dead to rights trespassing. You resisted arrest, fell and knocked yourself out. He released you because he wants to keep all his options open, Bob."

"Options?"

Doc turned off the lights.

"Sam might want to press murder charges."

❧

Doc pulled onto Main without checking for traffic, as if he knew no one would be in his way.

"You're looking very peaked, Bob."

"Who did I . . . ? Who was I supposed to have killed, Doctor? Can you tell me that?"

"The man in The Little Piney was Joe Pickens Junior," Doc informed me. "I can tell you that much."

"Joe Junior? He was . . ."

I stopped myself.

"Who identified him?" I asked.

"I did. Known Junior since he was born."

"Who found him?"

"Warnell Ames discovered the body. Facedown on the gravel shoal just south of the bridge over The Little Piney. Very near your home. Warnell walked up to Jacob Wells's place and Jake called the sheriff, who called me. While he was in the area, Sam decided to check on his property, that spread behind the cyclone fence on the other side of the river."

"We struggled?" I asked. "I fell and bumped my head. Sheriff Baxter put me in jail."

Doc nodded. "Pretty much like that, Bob."

"Warnell hasn't left Doker in years," I said.

Miss Ollie had told me that a hundred times, sniffed sadly about it a bit on several occasions when she misread my silence as sympathy. Her son didn't even know how to drive a car or even ride a bicycle.

"I have never once seen him down by the creek. Not in the ten months plus I've lived here," I told Doc Williams. "All Warnell ever does is sit on that stool and watch the Old Lion, looking out for Tammy Fay."

But Warnell was not out front of EAT as I spoke.

Miss Ollie, however, was staring out the front picture window but as Doc drove us past the café she backed out of sight and the OPEN neon above the entrance was extinguished.

When we were abreast of the Old Lion I asked Doc to stop. He did.

"Maybe Tammy's got my truck ready, Doctor, and I can save you a trip to Rushing."

The single garage work bay was empty, the rack lowered. Tammy Fay's tow truck was gone. I mounted the steps to her upstairs apartment and could see through a parted curtain that the upstairs apartment was its usual mess and seemed empty. Stank wasn't there either. Maybe the dog was still roaming the streets looking for some affection.

I got back into the station wagon, scratched the itch at the back of my head.

The doctor pulled onto Main Street without looking behind him, as was his privilege apparently.

"It just doesn't make any sense, Doc. What in the world was Warnell Ames doing at The Little Piney, that far from home?"

"Warnell said he was fishing."

"Fishing?"

"That is the story, Bob."

I scratched at my head some more.

"Who's going to tell Malcolm?" I asked. "About his daddy?"

"This is not yet for public broadcast, Bob. I shouldn't have said anything about this."

He sped out of Doker, only slowed when crossing the narrow bridge over South Slough, an elongated depression that was not quite a creek and not quite dry land but just perpetual thin mud with a bridge depended over it.

My very expensive binoculars were sunk in South Slough.

The doctor braked the County meat wagon and eased off the State Road and onto County Road 615, hurried down the dirt. The wind whistling by us was hot and dry.

"So, what killed Joe Pickens Junior, Doctor?"

We passed Pick's UPUMPIT! There was nobody in the yard and no lights on in the store. My truck was gone, so I guessed the Right Reverend Mean Joe Pickens Senior had had it towed off as he had done on several previous occasions.

"Gunshot killed Junior, best I can tell at the present moment. Very large caliber. In the back."

"I don't even have a gun."

"Well, Bob, you maybe might would think that is a point in your favor," Doc allowed.

"Malcolm's going to take this hard."

Doc shrugged philosophically.

"Malcolm sees what he sees, Bob, so the child can entertain some fantastic notions very seriously. He'll probably invent a story where his daddy's the hero," Doc suggested. "Anyway, I don't believe that Malcolm has seen Joe Junior in several years. Perhaps that will make the situation easier on him."

I was not sure about that. Whether it would make it easier or harder on Malcolm and whether the kid had seen his daddy recently or not. I suspected Malcolm had seen his daddy, down by the creek, indeed had been supplying Joe Pickens Junior with potted meat and cigarettes and Coca-Colas for at least a couple of days judging by the trash I had seen around the creekside fire pit.

"Was Joe Junior always a problem, Doctor?"

"He wasn't a 'bad kid,' if that's what you're asking, Bob." The doctor considered. "Junior was just a wee bit too stupid to be smart and a wee bit too smart to be stupid, if you understand what that means."

I nodded since the same might be said of me.

"Junior used to attend Melissa's summer camp, Camp Osage, along with pretty much all the rest of the cast of young characters around here and it was just remarkable how Junior could figure out games and crafts and get along fine with people and then he'd do something so stupid it would be remarkable. The main problem with Joe Junior was that he was just smart enough to get himself in serious trouble and too stupid to get himself out of it."

"Not like Warnell?"

"Warnell's intelligence is about on par with a box of hair stored in the back room," the doctor said. "But that is not his fault. Warnell was dropped on his head several times," the doctor said. "I actually once dropped him myself when he was just a few days old." Dr. Williams nodded. "But Warnell, defective as he is, has at least been with the program around here. Not like Joe Junior, who had to go off and do his own thing and never did get with the program around here."

"Never got with the program," I repeated.

"Some people just don't, Bob. Some people just stay stupid and don't ever get with the program and just won't change their ways." The driver looked sideways at me, then looked back at the road. "I won't mention any more names, Bob."

"People don't change much, do they, Doctor?"

"Unfortunately just a few things that I've noticed really change people, Bob—drug addiction, electroshock and the Conversion Experience. Not much else seems to make a fundamental difference."

"Including summer camp?"

"The women, my wife especially, thought they were making a positive difference in those kids' lives, Bob. I was hardly in the position to tell them they weren't. To look at those kids all grown up now you would have to say Camp Osage did not exactly turn out as the women planned."

"What does, Doctor?"

"Exactly, Bob."

The physician smiled nostalgically.

"But it did have its moments, Bob. Camp Osage surely did have several of those."

The graveyard going by on our right was a collection of upstanding white stones.

"What do you mean, Doctor?"

"It's not something I want to discuss right now, Bob. It really is local business, which means it is not your business and the only reason I have given you as much information as I have is to impress upon you the importance of personal space."

"Personal space?"

"You might want to expand yours, Bob. Say, to Hot Springs. I understand you are partial to Hot Springs."

"I see," I said.

The doctor stopped in front of the First Rushing Evangelical True Bible Prophecy Church of the Rising Star in Jesus Christ where these promises still held forth:

WELCOME ALL, SERVICES AT 8:30 AM SUNDAY, THE LORD'S DAY. THE CORRECT AND GOOD NEWS AS PROCLAIMED BY THE GOSPEL AND DELIVERED BY THE RIGHT REVEREND JOE PICKENS, SENIOR, MINISTER OF THE FAITH.

I looked at Doc. He seemed to be dismissing me.

"I just thought you maybe might would appreciate the little walk home from here, Bob. Stretch the old legs out."

I opened the door.

"Thanks for the ride, Doc. And the information."

"Hot Springs is nice, Bob. Just what the doctor ordered, I believe."

"Yes," I agreed. "Yes, it is, Doctor."

"Let a word to the wise suffice, Bob?"

"Sure, Doctor."

I got out of the ME's car, shut the door.

Doc drove off.

I headed home with that wise word ringing in my ears.

CHAPTER 9

I walked in the middle of the road. The blister on my heel was a dull throb.

Jacob Wells's cows in my unfenced fields shuffled and lowed. I stopped and threw rocks at them until my sore shoulder gave out, then I went on.

The air was hot in my lungs and my body was hot, flushed as if I had been working all day in the garden. Chinos chafed my legs and my T-shirt clung to me like a second, dirty skin. I peeled it off and wiped the sweat from my face, my scalp.

The late-summer sky was tilted fully at night, the gibbous moon inserting itself like a bookmark through a hazy, dark book of clouds.

My chickens would be glad to have me safely home. I heard their scratching on the warped boards of the front screenporch.

A dog growled when my loafers crunched on the driveway. I picked up a handful of pea gravel to throw, thinking it was one of the Wellses' mutts escaped their pens and gone awandering.

From the shadows under the porch hobbled a short-one-leg hound.

"Stank?"

The old bluetick barked once, bent her head into my knee, whined. I scratched her ass, looked up the sideyard and saw the scabrously rusted propane tank, saw my

Cadillac. And saw the gleaming grille of a big, well-tended tow truck.

"Tammy Fay?"

Stank hobbled toward her mistress's vehicle. I followed.

My mechanic was asleep in the front seat of her truck. Her arm was crooked and propped on the open window, the sleeve of her coveralls rolled up above her biceps to expose the white skin of her elbow.

The soft flesh on the inside angle of her left arm was tracked with the scars of intravenous drug use. Years' worth of heavy use and a fresh dot of congealed blood.

That didn't surprise me. We are all attracted to types.

Tammy Fay snored softly. Sweat sheened her upper lip.

My beat-up Ford pickup was still hooked and hanging by a thick steel thread from her tow truck.

Her head was tilted back on the bench seat. On the shotgun side floorboard was a stuffed-tight army-green duffel bag with glossy fashion and pulp *True Story* magazines piled atop it. A corner of a red leather suitcase poked from under a tarp on the tow truck's rear bed.

Tammy Fay's swollen lips were cracked and parted. I touched a fingerend to her bottom lip and she stirred, opened her puffy eyes.

I put the finger in my mouth, tasted salt and spit and cigarettes, savored the smell of her hair, of grease and oil and sweet skin.

She stretched. When she shook her hair out I saw the golden wedding band on the gold-link chain around her neck.

"You surprised me, Bob. I just came out to bring . . ."

I walked toward the back of the house.

"I just came to bring your truck back," she said. "Preacher Pickens called me to tow it, but I just towed it here instead of into town."

Those logistics did not sound likely.

I didn't turn around, just kept walking.

On the slab patio Stank was facing off with one of Jake Wells's sheep, squared nose to nose with a big ewe.

"Get her, Stank," I said.

The sheep bolted at the sound of my voice and the dog chased after her, well as the dog could on three legs, limping into the back field.

I mounted the steps, stopped on the back porch to grab a couple of beers out of the refrigerator, opened the screen door, switched on the kitchen lights against the darkness, let the screen door slam shut behind me.

I plugged the drain of one side of the double basin kitchen sink and filled it half full with cold tap water, dipped my dirty T-shirt into the water, soaked it loaded, squeezed it empty over my head. I screwed the cap off a beer and took a long draught, pulled the soggy stick-it note from Motel 6 out of the pocket of the wet T-shirt, reread the information there.

Leo King, 483 Babcock St., Arkadelphia, Arkansas.

An engine started up, the winch whined, but I didn't look out the kitchen window. I killed the beer, went to the front porch and checked on my chickens. Malcolm had fed them but I changed their fouled water. I returned inside, went into the bathroom and took a long, chilling shower, scrubbed myself, from head to toe with lye soap and a rough loofah, washed myself until I squeaked. Cleaned my fingernails, between my toes, every little nook and cranny of me, until I was clean as a whistle.

I figured Tammy Fay was gone.

Naked, I padded barefooted back into the kitchen for the other beer I'd left on the counter.

From the back porch the distinctive sound of a Zippo lighter unhinged with a *clink!*

Tammy Fay's face, behind the warped screen of the back door, was briefly illuminated as she lit a cigarette with a green G. I. issued Zippo. Her features were raised up and hollowed out by that small flame, the lines on her face, around her deep-set eyes, around her wide mouth, on her broad forehead, were grooved and deeper than I had seen them before.

She blew smoke through the screen between us. I put the beer down on the countertop.

"Hey," she said. "You. Bob."

I went to her straight as a divining rod to deep buried water. She put a hand against mine to hold it there on the screen and I could feel her palm hot through the wire mesh, feel her skin. Water dripped off my spine and a breeze went past us both, from outside to inside and it chilled me to a shiver.

She closed her eyes and pressed her lips together, dropped her hand from the screen and let me push the door open to her. I stepped onto the porch and put my hand on her face, open against her cheek, and she leaned into my hand and kissed my palm. That hand quaked and moved down her long neck, traced a line over the tanned triangle below her chin, fingered the zipper of her coveralls where her flesh was soft and encaved, hollow at the base of her throat, soft. I took hold of that zipper and dragged it down, over the gold chain, over the gold ring, between her breasts and to the cleft of her legs.

She was naked underneath.

The cigarette slipped from between her fingers, discharged sparks against my bare feet, burned my skin.

She bit her lower lip and swayed slightly backward and

then leaned into me, took my hand and guided it to her breast, put her mouth on my neck and bit into me.

"Tammy . . . ," I said because that was pretty much it for me at that moment, just her.

She bit my lip, drew blood.

"Shut up," she warned.

She dragged me down the back steps, to the garden where the dirt was crusty dry on top and wet underneath. Her coveralls were now undone to her waist and my mouth fell to her breasts, to her nipples, and she moaned and fell back on the dirt as I worked the coveralls off her, explored her skin, felt the scars on her arms and the scars on her back and ass, as I buried my face in her and tasted her, smelled her like the dirt. My tongue, my fingers tested her to the curved bone, drew a dry, hoarse scream.

In the back field a dog howled and a sheep bleated and the woman's breath rattled as she pulled me up on her, into her and forced her teeth into my shoulder.

Blood ran and her nails on my back were a rake. I augured into her and she moaned very loud as they do in pornographic films. The sky above us was distant and vaulted and, to me, there was nobody in the world but us for a moment.

Lights flashed, a star exploded and a hot breeze blew over the garden, to shake loose seeds from the fibrous, dried-out pods of okra. She dug her hands into my ass, raised her knees and pulled me deep, yelled, "Hard!"

I tried to be hard.

"Hard! Hard! Hard!"

Like that was not just a request but a statement of fact and meant something about the world maybe but nothing much, really, about me, Bob Reynolds, at all.

And then she shivered and cried out again, moaned and wrapped her long legs around my waist, her long arms around my ribs and crushed me to her, opened her eyes, finally, and looked at me, commanded,

"Come in me now."

And I did, like I hadn't for a very long time.

❦

She pushed me off, gathered up her discarded work boots her coveralls, went inside.

A minute later the shower came on and she screamed curses because there's no hot water in my house, just very cold water from a very deep artesian well.

❦

It was several minutes before I realized I was being watched.

Leaning on the hood of Tammy Fay's tow truck Warnell Ames, Miss Ollie's son, snickered.

A camera light flashed and he took another picture of me.

❦

She was standing in the kitchen, dressed in one of my white dress shirts, a pair of clean chinos cinched round her waist with my favorite necktie. It was the tie, red silk with a neat print of yellow, I'd worn for my momma's funeral and many years later for my own wedding.

A good necktie is a good investment.

Her boots were in one hand, a beer in the other. A cigarette dangled from a pouty lip.

I walked past her and into the bedroom where her dirty coveralls were tossed atop my dirty clothes pile. I dressed in a pair of cleaned and pressed chinos and a fresh-from-the-package white T-shirt, antifungal socks and one of my many pairs of sensible walking shoes, then returned to the kitchen.

She was leaning over the sink, staring through the screen into the sideyard.

"Warnell! You idiot, get the hell out of the driver's seat!"

"Warnell's not exactly a credible witness," I said. "Or a dependable accomplice."

She turned, leaned her ass against the counter, dropped her boots on the floor, dragged on her unfiltered coffin nail.

"You cannot even imagine, Bob." She sighed, blew out smoke. "Warnell doesn't even know how to drive a fucking car. Which has made things pretty complicated of late. But I do have a tow truck. And Warnell is big and strong. And faithful as a stupid dog. Has been forever." Tammy Fay seemed to reconsider her sidekick. "Actually Warnell, he's pretty handy. Idiot Warnell ties up loose ends pretty good, him just being him and being so faithful to me and all. He surely does."

"It's surprising what people can accomplish when you take full advantage of them," I suggested. "People can downright surprise you when you pressure them enough," I said.

"You take what you can get and work things out, don't you, Bob?"

"I suppose you do," I agreed. I had.

"Anyway a picture's worth the word of a thousand idiots, right, Bob? And the best insurance a girl like me can get is photographic evidence." She looked at me sideways. "Besides, do you think anyone wouldn't believe you fucked me if you had the chance? That you wouldn't be my sugar daddy if I let you? That you wouldn't do anything for me if you were my little john? Any crazy thing at all, Bob?"

These were more rhetorical questions, so I didn't answer them.

"You're smart enough to understand all this, aren't you Bob?" she asked me.

I wasn't sure if I was or if I wasn't.

"I don't care what everybody says about you, Bob. You are not the crazy stupid guy people think you are. You are actually pretty smart, aren't you, Bob?"

I said nothing to that backhanded compliment that damned me with faint praise, considering the local intelligence level.

"So?" she asked me. "What?"

The "so what" seemed to be (as far as I could ascertain it on available information) that in the very recent past Joe Pickens Junior had been hiding on the creek side of The Little Piney (with his son, Malcolm provisioning him) and Joe Pickens Junior had witnessed Warnell and Tammy Fay dumping Buck King's body into The Little Piney (for whatever reason they had to do that and on whatever day at whatever time, I didn't know), then Warnell (or Tammy Fay herself, though that seemed less likely) had probably also shot and killed Joe Pickens Junior, in order to eliminate Joe Pickens Junior as a witness (who might want to trade such eyewitness testimony about a murder one for a plea bargain on his own dope-dealing rap).

The timetable was hard to figure, but Buck was drowned sometime shortly after I coshed him unconscious. And then Joe Pickens Junior had probably been killed (and reported by Warnell, which seemed highly unlikely, but there it was) while I was in jail.

But I wasn't going to ask Tammy Fay if this was how it had played out.

She would tell me what she wanted me to know and

would not confess to anything she did not want to confess to. If she needed to implicate me in Buck's death or if she needed to pin Joe Pickens Junior's death on me, then she would try to do that. She would not hesitate to make me her scapegoat if I was the best option. That was plain.

"Poor Bob. Everybody in town knows you sit over there on Elm Street in the morning with your big ol' binoculars and your little old dick, jerking off in your truck behind Miss Ollie's azalea bushes. Even poor Miss Ollie knows you're obsessed with me," Tammy Fay said. She looked at me like as a dead catfish ready for the fishnet. "Stalker, is what you are, Bob. And everybody around here knows that because I have told everybody about it and even have pictures of you doing it. Poor Bob, jerking off in his truck when I open up my morning curtains for him."

"And you knew I was over there all this time, across the street from the Old Lion?" I asked. "Watching you. You never said anything to me about it."

"You never saw much, did you, Bob?" she asked.

"Just enough to keep watching," I remembered.

"I always thought you might wind up being useful for something, Bob," she said. "Though I also always knew I might have to let you come inside me to make you that useful."

I nodded.

"Well, Bob, was it as good with me as you always imagined?"

"Yes," I admitted.

Why not admit it?

"I didn't feel much myself, Bob. A guy like you can't really fuck a girl like me, can he?"

She said that without rancor, without much interest really, casually, as an ethnographic observation almost, which made it even worse.

But she said it. And it hurt me.

But I nodded.

She smiled, picked up the soggy stick-it note from Motel 6, smoothed it out on the countertop, exhaled through her nose.

"Oh Buck," she said to the sticky note. "I'm going to miss a real man's good hard fucking, you bastard."

She raised an eyebrow at me, baiting me though my rising was over with her.

"Husband?" I asked.

She ripped the note into shreds and stuffed the shreds into the drain of the sink, stuffed in her cigarette after them and ran some cold water over them.

"Why, Bob Reynolds, Buck King was an old man, just like you. Not quite old enough to be my daddy in the regular world, but he did not miss it by much."

"Was he your daddy?"

She moved her head. Her long hair was wet along the edges.

"Not in any biological sense," she said. She looked pensive then or something other than cruel. "I have had a lot of daddies, Bob. And Buck used to pretend he was Daddy sometimes. When I was especially naughty. But generally he was more the husband type, even though we never actually could get legally married since he's already married, has been since high school to his prom queen sweetheart." Tammy Fay laughed, sarcastically I thought, and touched the jewelry on her neck. "We traded rings though. A long time ago."

She touched the gold band chained around her neck, the one I had taken off the neck of the dead man from the creek, from around Buck's thick, red neck and that the High Sheriff of Poe County had taken back from me and given to Tammy Fay—the industrious black widow in my

great big rural route mailbox could not have constructed
a more elaborate web. And with the exact same amount
of consciousness.

"I see," I said. And I did see. I thought, at least, that I
understood a good bit now.

She gathered loose tobacco off her lip with her tongue,
then spit it out.

"Maybe you do, Bob. A fellow like you . . . Maybe you
do see how it is with some men, some people." Tammy
Fay nodded. "Buck, he just had this crazy thing for me.
From the time I was just little, he had a thing for me. Not
love, but something."

She started to work bare toes into a work boot.

"You know how that is, Bob?" she asked "Obsession?"

"I might," I said. "So what now?" I asked.

"So now, thanks to you, Bob Reynolds, I am a free
woman."

"Thanks to me?" I asked.

She nodded, slipped the other foot into the other work
boot.

"You delivered the blow with your binoculars, Bob. That
blow was not fatal, but it disarmed him enough so that
Idiot out there and me could deal with Buck. I hadn't been
able to deal with him for years and it was just getting
worse with ol' Buck."

"I understand," I said. I was a tool. I understood that.

"Hard to believe you could do it," Tammy Fay said.
"Hard to believe you had it in you. And it was very hard,
very, very hard to ever catch Buck unawares. But I guess
you caught him off guard and a righteous whack with a
pair of big-ass binoculars did the trick for us, didn't it?"

"You found him unconscious and that was a good
opportunity for you," I said. "And you are an opportunistic predator, aren't you, Tammy Fay?"

"It was a good opportunity, Bob. And yes, I am an opportunist, so I took advantage of the good opportunity you provided me with."

"I understand," I said. "Buck was getting to be a problem."

"I've been trying for several years now to get rid of Buck," she said. "You know how hard it can be to get rid of somebody who's in your life but weights you down so much, you feel like you're swimming in mud, don't you, Bob?"

I nodded. I did know about that perfectly well.

"But you have to get rid of them so you can move on with your life. Right, Bob?"

I said nothing, admitted nothing.

"But what with one thing and another I just never got around to getting rid of ol' Buck. That man was pesky and persistent. Has been for fifteen years." She shrugged a shrug that explained a lot.

"Why didn't you just leave?" I asked.

"You don't understand the situation around here," Tammy Fay told me.

She thumped the flesh of her inner arm and winked at me, explaining somewhat the situation.

"Something of a bird nest on the ground, you might say," she said. "Though the downside is way down."

"So you didn't leave because your drugs were here?" I asked.

"I didn't leave before now because the circumstances were never exactly right for me to leave before now. And, you don't know Buck, but Buck would have found me. He was the best bounty hunter in this part of the world. He would have tracked me down." She shrugged again. "And then who knows what would have happened. Me dead instead of him, probably."

"But the circumstances got right recently," I said.

She nodded.

"Exactly right, Bob."

"You saw your boyfriend Buck laid out, knocked out unconscious in his car and Warnell was right there to help load him on your truck and take him to the creek and dumped him in and you just couldn't resist that opportunity."

"Golden opportunities don't grow on trees, Bob," Tammy Fay said.

"No," I said. "They don't."

She sighed, sort of nostalgically.

"He was a good fuck, Bob. And Buck, he took care of me and my expensive little habit all these years."

She massaged the inside of her arm.

"But it was getting a little old, you know? I'm getting a little old, Bob. Fourteen years plus with that bastard was just too long with that bastard. Buck would never have let me go either. Not free and clear. He was just too crazy about it, you know? We were too connected. He couldn't just let me walk. That was never going to happen."

I nodded.

"And life's too short. You know what I mean, Bob? I was crazy about him for a while. When I was a kid I thought he was the one and only shit. He was a handsome bastard. And when he came back from the Corps I even let him get me hooked. Got that little master-slave thing going when I was a kid. But even that's got old. You know what I mean, Bob?"

"Yes."

Obsession can get old, even obsession can get old. And there arrives a time when you have just had enough. There are limits to patience, even the patience of a spider must wear out eventually.

"There are limits," I agreed.

"You do understand me, Bob."

"Better than you might imagine," I agreed.

She smiled, pursed her lips.

When she moved toward the door I grabbed her arm.

"Let me go, Bob."

"I thought you liked it rough."

She glared at me.

"Warnell!" she called for her bodyguard who hulked on the back porch.

I let her go, backed away.

She put her hand on the screen door.

"So now you're leaving," I said.

"To parts completely unknown, Bob. So, if you were thinking of following me, forget that thought."

"I wasn't. I wasn't thinking that thought at all."

"You're a smart boy, Bob. Not too pretty, but smart. And if I ever have need of you, I'll be in touch."

She pushed open the screen door. On the back porch steps, breathing heavy, Warnell waited.

She turned back to me.

"I've got to give Idiot here another hand job and then I'll be out of this country, Bob. Probably out of your hair for good."

"What about the sheriff?"

She raised an eyebrow.

"Who do you think the High Drug Lord is around here, Bob?"

I nodded.

"And Joe Pickens Junior?"

She shrugged.

"Joe Junior was always stupid enough to think he was smarter than everybody else, Bob. Or let me say Junior was always just smart enough to get in on the shit and then to just get the short end of it."

"So you, or Warnell, shot and killed Joe Pickens Junior? Did you find Buck King's gun and shoot Joe Junior with it?"

"Bob, really . . ." When Tammy Fay shook her head her honey-blond hair hid her eyes for a moment and then revealed them again, staring at me. "I said Joe Junior was stupid, I didn't say I was." She paused, then added, "Let's just say things worked out in a local way."

"Quite a place this place," I said.

"You cannot imagine, Bob."

She leaned against the screen door as if she were weary.

"Just to warn you, Bob. Because you are sort of nice, in a loser way. Buck's got to turn up. He is a respectable citizen in our community. He's a deacon in the Second Baptist Church. He has a wife and kids and clients, even lawyers and judges and doctors upstanding, who will ask questions. His daddy is Dick King, King of Tires."

"That could get sticky," I suggested.

She shrugged and did not seem too concerned.

"Sammy will take care of it. Sammy's good at stuff like that. And you'll be all right if you stay out of Sammy's way. He won't bother you, because you've got money and your own lawyers. But if any of you screw with me . . ."

"You've got pictures," I said.

"And I've got stories to go along with my pictures, Bob. All recorded. All safely hidden away here and there and everywhere." She looked at me again and raised a dark eyebrow. "And now you're in the pictures and in this story too."

"I am," I said.

She stepped off the back porch onto the slab patio and headed toward the tow truck.

"You ready for your hand job, Idiot?" she asked Warnell, who was drooling on the back patio, staring at her.

"Whole thing, Tammy," Warnell said. "I get the whole thing this time," he pleaded. "Just like him." He pointed across her at me, standing on the patio. He was fairly slobbering.

"We'll see about what you get when we get to the Slough," Tammy Fay said.

She walked to the truck with her lapdog leashed to her.

"Good-bye," I said to her.

She did not even look at me.

They left in the tow truck.

CHAPTER 10

She had forgotten half a crushed pack of Pall Malls in a pocket of her coveralls. I kept the cigarettes and burned the coveralls in the backyard trash barrel down to pure ash and a long metal zipper. For a long time I sat on the back steps smoking her cigarettes even though I do not normally smoke.

I had spent a lot of time sitting on those steps over the last few months, staring at my weedy fields, on the lookout for my neighbor's livestock, waiting for the sun to rise or set. Waiting for something to happen. Now something had happened and I waited for it to be over.

This too will pass, I told myself. Like all else, this too will pass and she will be gone, physically at first and then from my memory and eventually there will be nothing to remember about her that I don't care to remember because life is mostly memories and projections and so controllable, if your mind has the correct control dials.

I tried to pretend it was just another such time, a time that would pass as just another memory.

But then Stank limped out of the back field and started barking.

"Oh shit."

Stank whined.

"This is pushing it," I told the dog.

The old hound barked, then sniffed my crotch.

I did not want a dog.

"I have got my limits," I told Stank.

Stank barked hoarsely.

I raised my hand but could not hit her.

I walked off, toward The Little Piney.

Stank bounced after me. She was slow, but seemed persistent. I decided to let her run herself out, pick her up on the way back.

I had only walked a hundred and twelve steps when I saw Malcolm headed toward me, his arms worked like wings preparing for takeoff. He was shaking his head like his hair was full of bees. He closed the distance between us fast.

"He dead, Bob Reynold."

"I am sorry your daddy's dead, Malcolm," I said.

The kid stared at me.

"My daddy dead, Bob Reynold?"

"Shit."

"He is, Bob Reynold? Daddy dead?"

"I'm really sorry, Malcolm."

The kid brushed a hand over his nose, shrugged.

"Well, I guess I didn't 'spect no different from him, Bob Reynold. PaPaw always said Daddy'd wind up dead."

"I am sorry, Malcolm. I shouldn't have said anything. I just thought . . . you seem so upset, I just thought you had found out."

"I hadn't heard nothing 'bout that, Bob Reynold. Where I'm going to hear something? I only just saw Daddy yesterday 'round about this time of day down at the creek."

"Your daddy's been around awhile, Malcolm?"

"He come sneaking up to the store one late night lately, wanting me to steal some potted meat and crackers and cigarettes and money and bring it down the bridge. He was total busted, Bob Reynold, so I saw to feeding him, but I wouldn't be stealing no money from PaPaw."

The kid kept his moral compass handy like nobody else I knew.

"You knew why he was hiding out?" I asked

"My daddy, he always hiding out," said Malcolm. "Hid out day I was borned, PaPaw said. And never did quit hiding out from me since then."

"I'm sorry, Malcolm," I said, sincerely. "Your daddy did you a major misservice."

"Daddy that way, Bob Reynold. Never did trust Jesus Rising Star so he misservice everybody."

I wanted to give Malcolm a hug, but shied from that, waited. Malcolm seemed sort of stoical about his father's death.

"He's upset awful 'bout something yesterday and this last day I seen him, so I didn't 'spect nothing good come of it, Bob Reynold. I didn't 'spect nothing good from Daddy lately. Never did, tell the truth."

"I never expected anything much good from my daddy either, Malcolm."

"Then you know how it is."

I did.

"But I ain't getting no 'heritance money."

"I'll give you some of mine, Malcolm," I offered impulsively. "How about a thousand dollars?"

Malcolm considered.

"That about what you figure a daddy's worth, Bob Reynold?"

I nodded.

"I figure that's about what your daddy's worth, Malcolm Ray."

"All right then, Bob Reynold. Praise Jesus and I 'preciate you."

Stank hobbled up to us, sniffed at me, then turned to Malcolm, licked the boy's hand.

"This Miss TamFay's dog, ain't it, Bob Reynold?"

"It was. You want it?"

"I always did like this dog," Malcolm considered. "She ugly, but she a good dog."

Stank barked.

"Three-leg dog," the kid said. "Okay."

Malcolm nodded at me and the deal was done.

"I call her 'Three Leg' then. How about that, Bob Reynold?"

"Sounds right, Malcolm. I don't think that dog is smart enough to know the difference in names or in people either one." I motioned toward my truck. "Come on now and I'll take you back to the store."

Malcolm didn't move, kept his hand on the old bluetick.

I waited.

"It's something I didn't tell you yet though, Bob Reynold."

"What's that?"

"It's something down at the creek," he said.

"You saw something down at The Little Piney," I said. "Just now? In the middle of the night?"

"Yessir, Bob Reynold. I went down to find my daddy and bring him some stuff, but PaPaw on to me now and I couldn't get nothing to take him so I went down the creek to tell Daddy that but Daddy ain't there. But I did see somebody, pretty sure I did."

"What?" I asked. "Who?"

"If they both dead, Bob Reynold, maybe it's no use messing with it."

"But, you did see somebody down at the creek?"

"Yessir, Bob Reynold. Like I say, I was waiting on my daddy to show up but when he didn't I guess I fell asleep and when I woke up I heard that red-tail hawk crying out and I heard some splashing noises. For a second I thought it was my daddy, Bob Reynold. So I hollered out to him, thinking it was him down there."

He glanced down the dirt road as if there might be someone coming our way, a ghost maybe.

"You scared of something?" I asked him.

"Nossir, Bob Reynold. Ain't nothing to fear when Jesus be with you like the Rising Star."

I had my doubts about that but didn't voice them.

"There was somebody in the creek," I reminded.

"It was two mens, Bob Reynold. One standing over the other. The one looked at me and he throwed his hands up at the sky like he had been caught out."

"And the other man . . . ?"

"That man, he was down in the water, Bob Reynold, laid out like he was getting baptized, but he didn't have no robe on him and shirt on him neither."

Malcolm looked down the road again.

"That man down in the creek, I believe he was that man I seen at Miss TamFay's day or so ago, Bob Reynold. The one in the blood-red car. The one you hit upside the head."

I did not bother arguing this point with Malcolm again.

"I know who this man is too," Malcolm said. "Friend of the sheriff, name o' Buck's King. Bounty man, PaPaw tell me. Come after my daddy, because my daddy jump bails."

"You recognized him? Weren't you a ways off, Malcolm?"

"They was just near the bridge there, you know where the old down oak tree's at, right about in there. And I see good, Bob Reynold. You know about that. I can sure tell a man I seen before when I see him again. Even if he is dead. Or sitting up in his truck on Ellum Street."

"But who was the other man, Malcolm? The man over the dead man?"

"Bob Reynold, you know sometimes I sleep down by the creek. When PaPaw's mad at me."

Sometimes the kid slept with the chickens on my front porch as well, when his granddad's whippings got too severe.

"So?"

"PaPaw tells me I'm 'magining things, but sometimes I thought I seen him before," Malcolm told me. "An old man with a crazy beard down around the water. Wears hunting clothes with a orange deer hunting hat most the time. But this time he had on a red shirt with his orange deer hat."

"And it was this old man that was drowning the man you saw parked at Tammy Fay's place?"

Malcolm shook his head.

"Wasn't drowning him though, Bob Reynold."

The kid looked over his shoulder, then started walking toward my house.

"That old man was cutting his head off."

The truck wouldn't start. Not even a click from the starter.

"Shit."

The Cadillac, which hadn't been turned over in months, wouldn't start either.

"Malcolm, I'm going to walk up to the Wellses."

The kid hopped out of the truck bed. The dog hopped out too.

"I'll fix you truck for you, Bob Reynold. Me and Three Leg wait right here."

Faith Sue Wells was not going to let me in her double-wide trailer house.

Her dogs, penned on all sides of the house, were setting up a quadraphonic racket. Her twins, Isaac and Newton, hidden behind their mother's denim skirts, matched the dogs for howling. The woman stood in her doorway, jaundiced in bug light, steadfast as a courthouse statue of General Robert E. Lee.

"Faith Sue, this is a real genuine police emergency."

A twin poked his head out from between Faith Sue's hairy ankles.

"The thing is, Mr. Bob, it wouldn't be proper to let a man in the house at night without my Jacob being here. And he's over at Danielles shopping at the Piggly Wiggly right now."

"With due regard, Faith Sue, I am coming into your house and using your telephone. So please move aside."

"Well, the house is a mess," my neighbor apologized with a gross understatement, stepping aside. "We just in the midst of redecorating."

Apparently Jacob Wells's predilection for accumulation was infectious, interior as well as exterior and family-wide. Stuff I couldn't put names to was piled everywhere there was space for a pile.

A goodly bit of it was, or had been at one point in time, mine.

One of the twins (they were indistinguishable at a glance) picked up a dog-chewed dress shoe and looked ready to clout me with it, but the other kid got ahold of it and soon the pair of second-graders were tussling across a floor rug of mine I had bought in Turkey for almost five hundred dollars. The children tumbled out of the room, neither one of them uttering a syllable but energetic grunts.

The telephone was atop a pile of composting newspapers.

I dialed the operator and told her to connect me with the Poe County Sheriff's Department.

"You calling the Po-lice on us, Mr. Bob?"

My eavesdropping neighbor's disembodied voice filtered through trash and into the kitchen.

"I'm not calling Police on you, Faith Sue."

I hung up the phone, unsure of it now that it was in my hands and ringing.

"Jacob won't appreciate that, Mr. Bob."

"Got nothing to do with you or Jacob, Faith Sue."

"It's not very neighborly, Mr. Bob. We didn't mean nothing by what we took."

"I don't care what y'all stole from me, Faith Sue. I know all about that."

Maybe I should have forgotten the whole thing.

But Malcolm had seen the corpse in the creek.

"Mr. Bob?" the housewife called from the distance of another room.

"I'm still here, Faith Sue."

Thinking.

If I called State Police or the FBI, Baxter would be pissed enough to mess up my local life completely. As Smarty Bell had warned, the sheriff could plant drugs on me or in my place or in my vehicles, and screw me royal. Or worse. Kill me and have me bathing with the bigmouth bass just like that.

Tammy Fay said I would be okay: If I played ball.

I found a phone book and dialed a Doker number.

"Doc Williams here," my physician answered.

"Malcolm found another dead man in The Little Piney.

I imagine it's the son of your old friend from Korea, the bounty hunter named Leonard 'Buck' King."

"Malcolm found him," Doc repeated.

"Said he saw an old man cutting Buck King's head off. Would that old man be Baxter's daddy, your old friend, Samuel Baxter Senior?"

Doc cleared his throat.

"No telling what that boy will say, Bob. Malcolm Pickens is not a credible witness."

"You coming out here?"

"I will, Bob. Nothing to it, probably, but I'll be out shortly. You call anybody else about this?"

"I was considering calling the Staties, Doctor. Or the FBI."

"That wouldn't be wise, Bob," Doc said.

"I thought you might say that, Doctor."

Doc cleared his throat again.

"Bob, if I were you, I'd just vacate the vicinity for a while."

"Are you suggesting that a word should be sufficient to direct the wise out of town in this instance?" I asked.

"That's about it, Bob."

"Where would you suggest I direct myself to? Out of state? Out of county? Out of country?" I asked. "How far is far enough, Doc?"

"No need to be dramatic, Bob." The doctor was using his doctor's voice on me, making his orders sound like suggestions. "It's a very nice drive to Hot Springs this time of evening, for instance. Put the top on your convertible down, Bob."

"That top-down thing never worked for me," I admitted. "Since I don't have enough hair to blow in the breeze."

"Well, Bob, wherever you decide to go and however you decide to get there, just have a nice long stay . . ."

"A nice long stay away, you mean?" I asked, just to clarify.

"Yes, Bob."

"You mean don't come back for *a while*."

"Correct, Bob."

The good doctor seemed to be losing his patience with this patient, but I wanted as much information about his deal as possible as it seemed my life might depend on it.

"How long would 'a while' be?" I asked.

"You can be the judge of that," the doctor replied and hung up on me.

I guess I can upset even the most even keeled.

Malcolm was under the hood of the Cadillac, Stank beside him propped steadily on her three legs.

"I got to get going, Malcolm," I told my friend. "Like now. Like Right Now."

I stared at my truck. The hood was popped up in full extension and a wide array of mechanical-type things were spread on the ground around it like artifacts at an archeological dig.

"What happened to my pickup?" I asked.

"Bob Reynold, I tell you, it's been somebody messing with that truck of yours. Distributor wires all cut up, plugs pulled all out. Carb'rator off it. Issa mess in there. And idn't nothing I could do with all that mess, Bob Reynold. But I have the Elvis car started in about a second."

The Caddy had not ever run well, had not run much at all lately.

"If you can manage that I will much appreciate you, Malcolm."

I leaned into the pickup and opened the glove compartment, found my wallet. The cash was gone, but at least Tammy Fay had left the credit cards and the checkbook.

"You lookin' in a hurry to go, Bob Reynold, but you could cut me a check fo' my 'heritance first."

I headed toward the house.

"Thousand dollar, Bob Reynold!" Malcolm called after me "You remember 'bout my 'heritance I ain't got that you 'sposed to be givin' me?"

I walked into the house.

"I need me some 'heritance too," I heard Malcolm grumble behind me.

❧

I stuffed a package of new T-shirts into a grocery bag, with some clean underwear, an extra pair of walking shoes, my favorite short pants and some pressed chinos.

Still in the pocket of the dirty short pants I'd worn to the creek and that had not yet been cleaned were the XXL condoms and the cartridge I had found in the dead man's jeans, in Buck's back pockets.

I regretted not having used condoms with Tammy Fay—using both of these of Buck's would have been ironic—but sometimes it's difficult to be clearheaded and the big Trojans would not have stayed on me anyway.

I stuck the XXL Trojans into the back pocket of my chinos and also pocketed the cartridge and planned on dumping these off my property altogether by throwing them out the window as I overpassed South Slough, burying them in the sucking mud, alongside my binoculars.

I washed my hands very thoroughly several times, looked myself over in the mirror.

I still didn't look much different, looked pretty much the same as per usual.

And I guess I felt the same, more or less.

So, if anybody had been there to inquire about my state of well-being, I'd of said, "Fine," just like everybody else around here always does, sometimes even as they lay dying.

❧

I let Malcolm and Stank off at the First Rushing Evangelical True Bible Prophecy Church of the Rising Star in Jesus Christ. The kid wanted to pray for his daddy. I think he also wanted to thank Jesus for his thousand-dollar windfall inheritance.

I honked good-bye, reached under the front seat for my emergency Jim Beam.

The flask was gone.

In its place, snug in a nylon shoulder holster, was the biggest revolver I had ever seen in my life.

❧

The handgun was probably a foot and a half long and weighed maybe four pounds. The grip was black rubber, too big for me to comfortably hold in my small hand. I slowed the car, used a T-shirt to flip the cylinder open. All six chambers were empty. I slipped the finger-long cartridge out of my pocket, loaded the single bullet into one of the empty chambers.

The cartridge fit the revolver perfectly, so I figured it was the bounty hunter's gun in my hands.

Short of having "Buck" engraved on the barrel the revolver was a perfect match for the big man that had been

Tammy Fay Smith's sugar daddy (or whatever) since 1970 or thereabouts, the bounty hunter I had coshed on the head with my big binoculars in Doker and then found facedown in The Little Piney, breathing water, dead as a doorknob, and then who had disappeared only to reappear again.

I wiped the gun and reholstered it.

If I threw it out the window there it would be for anybody to find.

I shrugged, though there was nobody to see me do it.

I drove on.

There were headlights ahead on County Road 615 so I cut the Caddy's lights, pulled off the farm-to-market road and parked behind Pick's store, sat the car until Doc's meat wagon went by.

If I'd had a local lawyer maybe I would have called him for advice. But I didn't have one person in the world to trust.

And a whole world out to get me, it appeared.

A light went on in the store, then went off.

The gun beside me was about to burn a hole through the red leather seat.

I opened the door slowly, slipped out with the revolver, slunk eleven steps to Malcolm's snake pit, listened to their sibilant complaint. I wiped the gun completely with the tails of my T-shirt, tossed the firearm into the middle midsts of the pit, recovered the hole with the tarpaulin, then crammed the shirt deep in the burn barrel in Mean

Joe's sideyard, got in my car and backed up, eased onto the dirt road, took a right and headed down CR 615 to State Highway 7 and then the Interstate Highway and way out of there.

❧

Tammy's tow truck was parked well off the road near South Slough—a regular Local spot for sex and where she'd gone to give Warnell his hand job, I guessed.

If I had not been the cautious driver that I am and slowed as instructed going over the narrow bridge and not just caught the red wink of a lit taillight through the kudzu vines draping the trees around South Slough, I would have missed seeing Tammy Fay's truck altogether.

But, as History instructs us, it's what happens and not what doesn't happen that's History.

❧

Halfway between South Slough and Doker I saw Warnell slowly walking toward town. His head was down but he was moving at a good pace.

I drove past him like he was not even there.

❧

I cut my lights and took a back way into Doker and on Elm Street parked for a moment behind the azalea bushes. There was one streetlight in the town but it was blinking so erratically it could not provide any sensible directions— red yellow green green yellow red red yellow green green . . . so I drove past it.

The EAT sign above Miss Ollie's café was off, the neon-like strips of dark tissue burned on the brick, like slave scars, dark and raised like keloid.

The Old Lion was closed up and shut down, dark downstairs, but upstairs there were skittering shadows in a dim light like someone was in Tammy Fay's apartment with a flashlight.

With the Caddy's lights cut I wended my way out of town and onto a deserted back road. I switched on the car lights and drove slowly toward Bertrandville, came out near the parking lot of the Motel 6. I steered onto the interstate, aimed south and didn't stop until I was on the Lone Star side of Texarkana.

CHAPTER 11

I paid cash for a room at a new Motel 6 on Stateline Avenue near the interstate and did not leave the room for almost a week but to go to the liquor store and Waffle House. My room cost $14.95 a night.

There is nothing much more to tell about those days.

I watched TV incessantly since the motel had newly installed cable. I read newspapers. I drank. I slept. I tried not to worry as the newspapers and local and regional TV stations began to issue reports on the several deaths in the Doker, Arkansas, area.

At one point I decided that I knew all I was ever going to know. And if I didn't know everything, then there was likely nothing I wanted to know that I would ever be able or allowed, by Locals, to know.

And sometimes that's just the way it is: In strange lands, foreigners reach the limits of their Local Knowledge only as allowed by Locals and that is why foreigners are called Foreign and locals are called Local.

❧

Early the next week I bought another *Texarkana Gazette* and a *USA Today*, watched the TV news about the Ark-LaTex on KSLA and KSTB and watched the national news on all the several majors channels and even on CNN and since I did not hear much mentioned about the Doker deaths, I started to sober up.

Wednesday I checked out of the Texarkana Motel 6, drove back toward "home" only as far as Hope, where I checked into the Dew Drop Inn Motel, where I watched more of local and regional and national news on TV on the Three Major Networks (no cable at the Dew Drop), and read the *Arkansas Democrat* from front to back.

There was nothing about me in any of the reports, not about Randall Robert Reynolds or Bob Reynolds or "suspicious local man" or "wanted as a person of interest" so I continued toward my homeplace as far as Hot Springs.

I checked into the most reasonably priced room at the Arlington Hotel, which is right in downtown Hot Springs, Arkansas, and in my small room I read *The Sentinel-Record* from front page to back page and watched all the TV I could stand but did not indulge in sulfur baths or steam cabinets or hot oil massages or alcohol rubs, etc.

Still, nothing about me.

The next day I phoned the Crow's Nest for information, but Ladoris said Smarty Bell's girlfriend was a finalist in a Best Boobs and Bootie contest in Memphis and my favorite barkeep was in Tennessee to lend moral support to his girlfriend.

Doctor "Doc" Williams did not answer his home phone and there was only a machine at his office to answer my phone call, which machine I did not talk to.

There was modest mention of Leonard "Buck" King and Joe Pickens Junior still in the Press, but not nearly as much as you'd suspect there should be.

There was an article in the papers and on the newscasts about the drowning death of one Tammy Fay Smith, of Doker, Arkansas. Warnell Ames, of Doker, Arkansas, had been implicated in her death, the article said, and was under arrest.

But still nothing about me.

No mention of Bob Reynolds as part of that summer crime spree in Doker, Arkansas.

Thank you, Jesus, Rising Star.

I felt so much better about my current situation and the likelihood of my safely escaping it that I actually gave some thought to my abandoned chickens.

At least I thought about that poultry to the extent that I wondered if my chickens were faring well in the wide world or if they would be stinking dead on the porch by the time I returned since my chicken caretaker, Malcolm, now had probably cashed his thousand-dollar "inheritance" check and wouldn't need my ten dollars per week for taking care of my chickens.

But chickens die all the time, tens of thousands of chickens die every day, actually, by slaughter as well as by natural causes.

I bought a modest and reasonably priced bathing suit at a downtown drugstore and enjoyed the two-tiered swimming pool of the Arlington Hotel even though I did not get in the water. Friday and Saturday nights I had two drinks per night at the bar in the lobby. I listened to the jazz trio and watched a few couples dance, but I didn't ask anyone to dance and no one asked me to dance. In fact there was a lot more music that night than there was dancing.

❧

I slept most of Sunday and then Monday bright and early I headed to Doker. Back to Doker.

I pulled off the interstate at the Bertrandville/Doker/ Danielles exit and took a right. The Old Lion tow rig was parked outside RW King's Tire Palace, just a stone's throw from the near empty parking lot of the Motel 6.

I parked my Caddy beside her truck, went inside the tire store.

My heart was in my throat, as it will be when you think something that can't possibly happen might could happen. When the very strange notion becomes, for a moment of suspended disbelief, altogether probable. Maybe she was still alive.

There was a couple in the tool aisle of the Tire Palace Auto parts and Tire Store arguing over the merits of spark plugs balanced in the man's hands. The woman was pretty in an overdone way and wanted the best plugs. The man was unattractive and out of shape and did not want to spend a penny more than he had to. His necktie was silk, yellow and covered in a neat pattern with smears of red and it swung like a long pendulum over his short little pot belly. His bald head gleamed under fluorescent tube lights that crackled and hissed as if they were frying themselves.

I realized the man part of this couple looked very much like I must look in the world.

Behind the long counter at the back of the store a myopic old man flipped through a thick parts book, intent on its study as a divinity student studying the lineages in the Old Testament.

Nearby his elbow radiator hose coiled on itself like a snake.

I cleared my throat.

The man flipped another tissue-thin page.

"Excuse me," I said. "You know the woman that owns that tow truck parked out front?"

"Nope."

"You don't know her?"

"That girl never owned that rig. Dick King loaned it to her for decoration and tax purposes. She owed us money."

"You're not Dick King?" I asked.

"I'm not any kind of King. I just work here," he said. "Who are you?"

"I was just a client of hers. Over in Doker. She worked on my truck."

He flipped another page in his catalog.

"She worked on your truck," he repeated.

He sounded acutely skeptical. He had not looked at me yet, but then he did.

"Yes," I said.

"She wasn't a mechanic."

"No. She wasn't a very good mechanic," I admitted.

He squinted at me.

"You're serious," he said, repeated himself. "You're serious, aren't you?"

I shrugged.

"You actually paid her," he asked, "to work on your vehicle?"

I nodded.

He shook his head before he nodded.

"Well, you're the one she got the parts for then, so I guess you can pay Dick King for those parts she ordered."

"How much?"

He told me and I handed over my credit card.

"You knew she was . . . a working girl, didn't you?"

"I didn't know anything about her," I lied.

He assayed me, nodded.

"Well, if she ever serviced more than your vehicle, I'd have a blood test pretty quick. When they autopsied her she was positive for everything in the book, I heard. Half the sporting fellows in the Arkansas River Valley are tearing their hair out right about now."

"I don't need it," I lied. "But I appreciate the advice."

I guess I should have registered her death more, just for form's sake. But it was not really news to me and I didn't feel like making a show of grief about her, so I didn't do it.

"Just a word to the wise." The old man looked at my credit card. "Mister Reynolds."

I headed for Doker, switched on the eight-track player in the Caddy, inserted an old tape my wife had given me.

John Lee Hooker was having some troubles of his own. But, in the end, he was a peace-loving man and would rather leave and just say good-bye.

Good-bye.

CHAPTER 12

I steered the Cadillac beside the pumps of the Doker Exxon station. The attendant strolled over, ran an appreciative hand over the hood of the car.

"Fill it, please. And she's low on oil," I said. "I'll be back in a little bit."

I passed by a fellow sitting up under a tarpaulin sunshade selling watermelons off a flatbed and we traded quick comments on the heat, said how dry it was lately, how abnormal it was to be so dry in this part of the country where humidity was the most usual rule of the day.

I didn't stop more than that to talk to the watermelon seller, but kept on walking down the street until I got to the Old Lion Filling Station, which had been Tammy's Tune-ups and Towing.

The CLOSED sign was hanging on the inside of the office door. The work bay of the garage was empty. I walked around the building; half circled it slowly, climbed up the back stairs and peeked into the apartment through a torn curtain.

From what little I could see Tammy Fay's place had been overturned thoroughly.

I guessed somebody had been looking for her photograph collection.

The door was fastened tight.

I felt eyes on me and when I looked around I saw

Miss Ollie watching me through her diner's front picture window.

I descended the stairs and walked across the road that was a State Highway in general but our Main Street in particular, and stepped into EAT, stepped inside the cold café, sat in my regular booth, which gave the best view of the Main Street, the crossroads signal light, the Old Lion, of Doker, Arkansas.

Nobody local was there but me; but there was a table at the far end of the room filled with tourists, the men and the women all dressed in more or less the same outfit, in golf shirts and khaki short pants, all wearing walking shoes as ordinary and sensible as mine if less expensive than mine.

They talked in low voices and occasionally looked my way from behind raised-up menus as if they knew me or knew something about me.

The women were all shaking their heads "no" and the men were all nodding "yes."

But I doubt those tourists did know me or know anything about me.

Miss Ollie Ames put a cup of coffee with cream and sugar in front of me, though I prefer my coffee black and unsweet and always have.

"Hello, Mr. Reynolds."

"Miss Ollie," I said politely.

"A blue plate, Mr. Reynolds? Chipped beef today. Your favorite."

"That would be fine, Miss Ollie," I said, though chipped beef was not my favorite by any longshot.

But she made no move to serve that meal.

"I saw you over at the Old Lion, Mr. Reynolds," Miss Ollie said. "Just now," she said. "I guess you don't know, do you, Mr. Reynolds? That they arrested my son."

I looked out the front picture window, where Warnell

was usually sitting on his stool looking out for his mistress and waving at every passer-by.

"I read it in the Hot Springs paper, Miss Ollie. Her death was recorded in *The Sentinel-Record,* though there weren't many details except that Warnell had been arrested for her murder."

Miss Ollie looked past me into the day beyond the dusty plate glass of her front window.

"I haven't been to Hot Springs in a long time, Mr. Reynolds," she told me. "A very long time," she added. "How is Hot Springs these days?"

"Fine, Miss Ollie," I said. "Crowded, though. Lots of tourists. And it's hot this time of year. Very hot."

"But I should get down there again, shouldn't I, Mr. Reynolds?"

"Hot Springs is worth the trip, Miss Ollie," I said. "But not this time of year."

"Autumn is such a nice time to go to Hot Springs, though, isn't it, Mr. Reynolds?" Miss Ollie asked me. "When the fall foliage is out."

"The foliage," I said, "is beautiful then, Miss Ollie. Around Hot Springs in the fall is like being in a painter's palette."

Miss Ollie sighed, a little overdramatically, I thought.

"I guess I should plan on seeing that then, Mr. Reynolds? Hot Springs in the fall?"

"I guess you should, Miss Ollie," I said.

"Can you guarantee that, Mr. Reynolds?"

Miss Ollie ran a dishtowel over a tiny puddle of water that was on the booth table nearby my hand.

She had painted her fingernails, inexpertly, blood red.

My appetite disappeared much as the water under her dishtowel had disappeared.

"She owed me almost three hundred dollars in food tabs, Mr. Reynolds," Miss Ollie told me. "Does that seem right to you? To owe somebody what you never intended on paying, like she did?"

"Put what she owed you on my tab, Miss Ollie. Whatever it is."

"I couldn't do that, Mr. Reynolds."

"I've got plenty of money, Miss Ollie," I told her, repeated myself so that she would understand me. "I've got plenty of money for the right things, Miss Ollie."

"All right then, Mr. Reynolds."

I sat very still.

Miss Ollie made no move either. I could see the pulse in an artery in one of her dishwater hands that clutched a dishrag fiercely. I looked out the window at the Old Lion.

"Did you know her well or long?" I asked.

"I'm not sure anyone ever knew her well, Mr. Reynolds. But I have known her or known *of* her since she was a child." Miss Ollie raised a vague hand over her shoulder. "She was raised over in Danielles though. Raised in Danielles, in those trailer houses behind the Piggly Wiggly. Did you ever shop over there, Mr. Reynolds, at that Piggly Wiggly in Danielles? A lot of men do, I hear."

I lied, shook my head firmly against that even being a remote possibility.

"I try to stay as local as possible, Miss Ollie," I said, though truthfully I had visited Piggly Wiggly in Danielles on a few occasions.

Miss Ollie nodded, but slightly as if I were not particularly convincing.

"Her foster parents in Danielles or Social Service or whoever was in charge of her at that time used to send her away for the summers, over here to that Osage Camp, as they called it. Leave her over here all summer."

"Tammy Fay?" I asked, though I knew who she was talking about. "Was sent by her foster parents or Social

Service or whoever was in charge of her, to Camp Osage, which was the project of Dr. Williams's wife? The kids' camp that Melissa Williams ran?"

"Yes, Mr. Reynolds. In fact, she often lived summers with the doctor and his wife and then lived in Danielles the rest of the year with various foster parents and this went on for many years."

"Tammy Fay," I said, since Miss Ollie seemed unwilling to say the young woman's name.

"Yessir, her." Miss Ollie brushed a fly away from her face. "And then the doctor gave her the Old Lion to stay in when she turned twenty-one and she moved in there permanently, more or less. That was about five or six years ago, Mr. Reynolds. Right after the doctor's wife passed on."

I tried to position all the players in this longstanding local drama.

"So Warnell knew Tammy Fay from Camp Osage?"

"My poor son, Mr. Reynolds," Miss Ollie said. "His head was twirled like a top until it was spun off by that girl. Like all the rest, but Warnell was the worst smitten. Followed her around like a puppy dog, whining after her affection. He would do anything for her. She made him eat dog poo once in front of a bunch of other kids from camp."

"Why?" I asked, even though I did not need to ask.

"Just because she could," said Miss Ollie. "You know that as well as I do, Mr. Reynolds. It was pathetic."

I looked at Miss Ollie in the face and she blushed.

"And now Tammy Fay is dead," I said.

"She was a force of nature of sorts, Mr. Reynolds. Like a terrible storm. But even a tornado blows itself out eventually."

I said nothing as this seemed to sum things up pretty well, save for the aftermath.

"I couldn't blame anybody?" Miss Ollie asked me. "Could you, Mr. Reynolds?"

"What do you mean, Miss Ollie?"

"Could you blame anybody in this business, Mr. Reynolds?"

After a pause, I said, "No, I couldn't, Miss Ollie."

But somebody had to take the fall for all this business.

"I am really sorry for your own troubles in all this, Miss Ollie."

"You cannot imagine what I have been through, Mr. Reynolds."

"It's a shame for you, Miss Ollie."

"Things have to work out somehow, Mr. Reynolds."

"It's an admirable philosophy, Miss Ollie."

We were very still for a moment, Miss Ollie was and I was. The tourists at the other end of the room chewed their food loudly and leaned toward me and Miss Ollie.

"There's just some people you're better off not having around, Mr. Reynolds. I was not one who wished her harm. She had a bad time of it too, like most of the rest of us around here. But she was no good to have around here. No good for anybody. Not back then. Not lately. Not ever."

Miss Ollie wiped a hand over her lean face.

"A girl like that is always no good in a place like this place, Mr. Reynolds."

A few wisps of soft gray hair escaped Miss Ollie's hairnet and she tucked them back with a move that made her tragic and almost pretty in a minor sort of way.

Ollie Ames was just a bit older than me, I realized. Or maybe even my own age.

"It's bad chemistry, Mr. Reynolds. It goes against natural order."

"I won't argue with you about that, Miss Ollie," I

agreed, since so much of the trouble in the world was just that, bad chemistry of one sort or another.

"It's better just to take what plain thing God gives and be satisfied with it, Mr. Reynolds. Folks try to be something they're not and never can be and try to have something they can't have and never will have. Don't you think that's true, Mr. Reynolds? That people reach too high? That people expect too much out of life?"

I drank my too-sweet and too-light coffee, wiped my mouth on a paper napkin.

"I won't disagree with you, Miss Ollie."

Though maybe Miss Ollie was totally wrong because if we only stayed in our natural states obeying natural orders we'd all still be living in caves, scratching crude symbols on rock, believing in gods and ghosts. Expectations could ruin us, but where would we be without them except always in the same old shit, in a cave battling shadows.

"I am right, Mr. Reynolds."

I nodded just to keep the peace. I was not in an argumentative mood with the world right then. After all this "business," as Miss Ollie had named our recent local trials, I was, truly, grateful to still have my hide even if I did not have any much hair to go along with it.

"I think I'll just skip eating right now, Miss Ollie. Tab up my daily blue plate though. Add Tammy Fay's bill to my running tab as well. I insist."

Miss Ollie did not argue with me on this fiduciary point again.

"As you like it, Mr. Reynolds."

I slid out of my booth, stepped to the door.

"They're talking about the death penalty for him, Mr. Reynolds," Miss Ollie said as she followed me. "It's an election year and the district attorney is going to seek the death penalty for my poor son. But the moratorium will save him, won't it?"

"I don't think anybody's going to be penalized to death in this country for quite a few more years, Miss Ollie," I said, though once the national moratorium was lifted on capital punishment I imagined Warnell would be on the list for lethal injection in Arkansas, even if he was brain damaged. Unless he got some powerful good lawyers.

The tourists called for their check. But Miss Ollie stayed focused on me.

"My son doesn't deserve the death penalty, does he, Mr. Reynolds? We don't deserve that, do we?"

I opened the door.

Warnell's three-legged stool was still on the slab porch.

"*You* don't deserve it, Miss Ollie," I said.

"Thank you, Mr. Reynolds. Thank you so much for saying so. It means the world to me to hear you say that."

"Whatever I can do then, Miss Ollie."

"I appreciate you, Mr. Reynolds."

I nodded.

"And I appreciate you, Miss Ollie."

When I stepped from the cool of the inside to the heat of the outside my brain seemed to spin, for a brief moment, like a top.

⁂

There was a pretty, but new girl at the checkout at Goody's Grocery—An Affiliated Foodstore and she was unfamiliar with me and so would not let me cash a counter check for cash money.

"I'll have to go get Mr. Goodman for approval."

"I'll go get him," I offered.

The line at the checkout was backed up, the girl was flustered and her cash register was beeping angrily.

Her neck was long and white and covered in hickies of various stages of bruising.

"Goody in the back?" I asked.

"Yessir."

Clarence Goodman was in what he hopefully called The Deli, a couple of plastic tables with attendant plastic chairs beside the butcher counter. He was eating from a family-size bag of low-fat potato chips. The remnants of a very large cut-meat sandwich littered the table. His chins were all greasy.

I put the counter check in front of him and he pulled a ballpoint out of his overpacked shirt pocket and scribbled his mark on the back.

"Shawnda's new," he apologized, returned the check to me. "We're just breaking her in."

"Mr. Goodman," I thanked him.

"We appreciate your business," he acknowledged, plunged back into his big bag of chips.

The checkout girl cashed my check and I walked across the parking lot of the grocery store and stopped at the watermelon seller.

"Hot one," he said.

"It is a dry heat, though," I replied.

"Unusual for these parts," he said, repeating our earlier dialogue near exactly.

You'd have thought we'd no memories to hear us talk and maybe that's the way to be. To forget what you can forget. To forget what you say so that you can just say it again over and over and over.

To forget what you've done so that you can do it again or won't need to do it again.

I paid for a watermelon.

"I'll come back in a minute," I said, looked across the street. "Pick me out a good one."

"Doker special," the watermelon seller said and winked at me. "Firm, but sweet."

I stepped across Main, stepped inside Dr. Williams's office.

Nurse shoved aside the frosted glass of the cubicle when she heard the front door open.

"Mr. Reynolds."

I nodded.

"Is the doctor in?" I asked.

"No, he's in Bertrandville testifying at the grand jury hearings. Then he's taking a little time off. Traveling to the Gulf Shore, I believe. And so I am not expecting him to return to the office for several weeks."

The certificates and diplomas, the photographs in the doctor's reception room were gone. The walls of the physician's office were freshly painted institutional green.

"Could you still set me up with an appointment for a blood test, please, Nurse?"

"I can do that, Mr. Reynolds. Monday at your regular time?"

"That will be fine, Nurse."

"You have been entirely negative for ten months, Mr. Reynolds. Are you looking for something in particular?"

"I am paranoid," I said. "I appreciate your understanding, Nurse."

"I'll put you down for next Monday, Mr. Reynolds. Your regular time."

"Can I get another prescription for my pills, Nurse?"

I had been without them for many days and my nerves had not much suffered that lacking, but it is reassuring to have medicine handy for what might ail you.

"That's not something I can do for you, Mr. Reynolds. And Dr. Williams has told me that it is not something he feels comfortable continuing. So perhaps you had better find another physician to prescribe your medications as he sees fit. I'll make you an appointment at Northwest Arkansas Regional Medical Center, if that's suitable, Mr. Reynolds?"

I nodded.

"Is there something more I can do for you, Mr. Reynolds?"

"You could tell me the local gossip, Nurse. Do people know how Warnell killed Tammy Fay?"

"Excuse me, Mr. Reynolds?"

"How did Warnell Ames kill Tammy Fay Smith?" I repeated.

Nurse cleared her throat.

"He beat her and then raped her and then left her near South Slough. Then he went and sat on his stool in front of the café until his mother found him and Miss Ollie called the sheriff who came and arrested him."

"The beating killed her?"

"No, the beating did not kill her. She rolled into South Slough somehow and drowned in the mud, Mr. Reynolds. Or else he pushed her, which seems most likely."

She had drowned in the mud, though this was not news I had read in the papers.

"Drowned in the mud," I repeated.

"Yes, Mr. Reynolds. She was found facedown in the mud of South Slough. If Warnell had only left her on dry land she would have survived, the doctor said. But apparently Warnell pushed her face into the mud while she was unconscious and she asphyxiated. Doctor Williams was very upset about it."

"So, Warnell confessed?"

"Eventually he did, Mr. Reynolds. To the High Sheriff. It took a few days of persuasion but he did confess."

"He confessed to Sam Baxter?" I asked for clarification.

"But it wasn't the sheriff that convinced him," said Nurse. "It was his dear mother, Miss Ollie, saint that she is, who finally persuaded Warnell to confess his sins and make a clean breast of it. For the good of everybody. For the good of the community."

"So Warnell confessed to killing Tammy Fay?"

"Eventually he did, yes, Mr. Reynolds."

"But not at first?"

"The gossip is that at first Warnell only confessed to hitting Tammy Fay because she wouldn't . . ." The nurse blushed slightly. " 'Go all the way' with him is the way he put it. He knocked her out apparently."

"Then later on he confessed to killing her? Beating her, then drowning her in the mud of South Slough?"

"Apparently it took some persuasion to get him to admit that he beat her at all beyond the one blow that knocked her unconscious. He never admitted to raping her. Insisted she promised him to 'go all the way' and so that was all he was doing—getting what he had been promised."

I nodded because I understood.

"And it was Warnell's mother, Miss Ollie, who convinced him to confess to more than that?" I asked.

"Yes, Mr. Reynolds. Warnell confessed to Tammy Fay's murder by drowning, but he never would confess to the rape. He did confess to the rape and murder of a lady tourist from several years ago. And he might not be done confessing yet. He has been crazy all his life, so there is no telling what else he might be responsible for." The nurse paused. "I'm sure he'll get the death penalty, won't he? Even though he's pretty retarded?"

"I believe there's a moratorium on capital punishment

just now," I informed. This was something I knew because it was something I had thought about in the last several years. "Without smart lawyers, Warnell will probably be lethally injected, eventually, even if he's mentally retarded. But that will probably take a few years."

"Unless that liberal governor we got pardons him," said the nurse with some heat.

I did not ever want to get into political discussions, but I said, "I don't see that happening, Nurse. Not if there are any bigger elections on the offer for the current governor."

"Warnell will probably like prison," the nurse said after a thoughtful pause. "I'm sure the food in prison is no worse than Miss Ollie's is at EAT. And all he ever does is sit around anyway."

"That's not quite all he did," I said.

In fact, Warnell had taken care of local business that summer. He had settled some complex affairs with his simple presence.

And if that did not seem exactly right—that it should all fall on Warnell Ames—it did not seem exactly wrong either. Particularly if he had really raped and murdered a tourist at some point in the not-so-distant past.

Sometimes there are extant in the world simple solutions to complex problems, not more or less improbable than the rest. The Greek tragedians had their God Machine. In Doker, Arkansas, that summer, we had Warnell Ames.

I went to the door.

"We'll see you next week then, Mr. Reynolds, for your blood test," Nurse said to my back. "Regular time. And I'll get you set up at Regional Medical Center for your medications."

"Thank you, Nurse."

"You're welcome, Mr. Reynolds. You have a nice day."

The Cadillac had been parked in tree shade near the Exxon station. The watermelon seller touched the corner of his eye as I approached then pointed at my car. In the shotgun seat there was a melon, light skinned, veined dark green, oblong, probably ten pounds worth of red meat.

I got in the fin tail, rolled all the windows down. The pump jockey came out of the Exxon station. I handed him a twenty.

"She was low three quarts."

I handed him another twenty. He went off to get change.

The watermelon seller stepped up beside me.

"Me and T. Bo, we was just saying this is quite a ride you got yourself here, Mister," the watermelon man said.

"Thanks."

"Wouldn't want to sell or trade, I don't suppose?"

I shook my head.

"It was my wife's car," I said.

"Good divorce settlement, huh? Me, I didn't get but heartache and assache from either first two times and on number three probably won't get much better."

"My wife died."

"Oh. Well, sorry to hear about that."

"She drowned in the bathtub."

The pump jockey returned from the office and handed me my change, which was short by a couple of dollars by my calculations.

"You hear about that, T. Bo?" the watermelon seller asked the station attendant.

"What's that, Kendrick?" asked T. Bo.

"Poor man says his dear wife drownt in the bathtub."

T. Bo took off his gimme cap and wiped the sheen off his bald head with the cap and put it back on, all the while eyeballing me.

"Ain't that a strange shame," T. Bo said.

I blinked and drove out of the shade and into the sunshine.

As I passed over South Slough I felt a tug at my belly like you will get when you're coming home from a trip, a nervous apprehension that is really the hope that everything is at home exactly as you left it battling the certainty that it is not.

Our bellies often remember what our brains forget.

I stopped at Pick's UPUMPIT! for bread and milk and my mail.

UPUMPIT! was closed, locked up tight as a drum. The handwritten sign on the front screen door said, "Went to Memphis. Be Back on Next Sunday for Regular Church Service."

I walked around to the sidelot.

Malcolm had cleaned out his snake pits, let the reptiles loose to fend for themselves while he was on holiday probably, released them so he could catch them again or else sold them all off to the snake-handling Christians who practiced their faith on the other side of the Grays or killed and skinned them for his wallet-making business, though I did not see any fresh snakeskins nailed to the back wall of the store.

The gun I had thrown into the snake pit was gone from the snake pit.

———

I parked the Cadillac on the edge of the cemetery, strolled over to see the freshly whittled crucifix cross that was planted in the freshly turned grave dirt on the Pickens plot. The orangewood above Joe Pickens Junior was still splintered from its very recent carving. Since the Right Reverend had been carving that cross while his son Joe Junior was still alive, I wondered if Mean Joe had predicted Joe Pickens Junior's fate or caused it.

In the well-tended Baxter plot Frances Mary Baxter was interred under a spray of new tea roses, still waiting patiently for her husband Samuel Baxter Senior.

The Wells Twins had rearranged the nativity scene in their front yard and decapitated a couple of the Magi and now were strategically located amongst the dusty men throwing clods of brick-hard red clay at one another.

Stank was asleep in the shade under the manger.

The twins threw dirt clods at my car until they couldn't throw far enough to make that fun.

My chickens had been let loose, were free ranging around the yard, appeared little worse for wear after my days away, but seemed glad to see me. They clustered around my feet and pecked at the laces on my walking shoes as soon as I alighted from the Caddy.

I counted twelve birds left from my baker's dozen, but could not figure which one was missing since they all looked the same to me.

The dead one I found later in the backyard trash barrel, dismembered by hand not knife it appeared, ripped apart and somewhat defeathered, beheaded and half charred.

The handiwork of the Wells kids probably, practicing their torture methods.

The screen door of the front porch was propped open with a rocking chair and there was still a scatter of feed in the troughs. The water in the birds' water feeders was fouled thick and gray with their own shit.

I changed the straw in the chickens' roosts and restocked their feed troughs and freshened their water dishes and hosed down the porch floorboards.

My house too was a bit overturned inside, the couches cut open strategically in several spots, chairs upset, my neatly typed pages of poetry disarranged, my clothes off the hangers, shoes mismatched, drawers pulled out.

This mess could have been attributed to either the sheriff searching for something or credited to my neighbor Wellses making themselves at home or as payback if Jacob thought I had called the cops on him.

I didn't miss anything if it was gone. I think I'm getting to be more like that about things in general, which I take as a good sign.

There was a longish missive, crudely handprinted in pencil on the torn-off cover of a paperback, thumbtacked to the back door.

"Deer Bob Rinald," the note from Malcolm read.

Me an Pa Pa went off to Memfs bekas we did
git sum mone frum my dadde aftr all. PaPaw
had him in surd aginst deth, so we got sum
mone aftr all. An plus you mone. Praze Jesus
Risin Star we wont even loos the church. Praze
Jesus. Everthing wrok out gud. An dadde had
a nice foonrl. I put food for the chikens in the
dishs but Papa sayed leaf the door open so I
did. Hop thas ok. I lef 3leg with jakowbwells
kid sins you was gone off. Sumbode sayed you
mit not cum bak but I hop you do or els I wil
mis you if you dont. You no I wil. Hop you had
a gud tim.

I am.
Malcolm Pickens

ps I foun sumthin with my snaks. Dint want to
loos it but Pa Pa syed I cudnt kep it aroun so I
put it in a saf plac I think. You wil find it wen
you git hungre. a hint.

The bounty hunter's big sidearm was in the refrigerator,
wrapped in a red mechanic's rags.

I got a beer and started straightening up my house.

CHAPTER 13

I waited until almost dusk to walk to The Little Piney.

I packed Leonard "Buck" King's revolver, still swaddled in rags, into a plastic grocery bag with a couple of beers and a flashlight. I put on my favorite short pants and my favorite pair of walking shoes and a fresh-from-the-package white cotton T-shirt, gathered the chickens onto the front porch and locked them in, started toward the creek.

I didn't expect to see anybody on County Road 615 and I didn't.

I felt something gathering on me as I walked, like a second skin that needed to be sloughed off. Sweat probably. The air had thickened while I was gone, was heavy now with humidity. There was no rain in the forecast, no clouds in the sky, but I could feel the rain ready to come soon and the clouds gathering. The fields whispered as a hot breeze shifted the Johnson grass.

I wiped my face on my shirt and walked on. The Grays shouldered against the bruised sky. The sharp granite ridge was just tinged red by the westering sun when I reached the bridge.

It seemed the right place to lose that killing piece of Buck King's, in the water where he had died. If the water had claimed the man's life.

I didn't know and probably never would know and did not care how Buck King had died.

Dead is as dead does. And the fit survive for whatever reasons they have, whatever reasons they need, serve whatever purpose they serve by staying alive.

And the best proof that things are as they should be is that they are that way.

I unwrapped the revolver, wiped it with the rags and meant then to throw the gun immediately into the water under the bridge over The Little Piney. The water was not particularly deep around there, but it was probably deep enough.

But the weight of the revolver in my hand seemed perfect. But the gun invited holding. But deadly things are meant to be caressed.

Threatened.

Tempted.

My momma had her alluring but vindictive god.

My daddy had his Jim Beam, his business.

My wife, her heroin, me.

I spun the cylinder of the revolver. When it stopped I spun it again and when it stopped again I held the gun with two hands and eased the long barrel of the revolver into my mouth then fingered the trigger.

The old man was a surprise.

"I knew you'd come back," he said.

He stood on the south side end of the bridge, the side his compound, his home was on. He was dressed in crusty, piss-stained pants, with a blaze orange watch cap on his pile of wild gray hair. He wore the red cowboy shirt of the corpse in the creek, Buck King's shirt. His beard was gray and twisted.

The giant yellow tomcat squatted near the man's bare feet.

I stopped breathing.

The barrel of the gun rattled against my teeth.

I pulled the revolver slowly out of my mouth.

The old man stared at me, did not blink. His eyes were vacant and hazy blue as a mad summer sky.

He moved very slowly forward.

In his hand was a very big knife, Buck's knife probably. The cat hissed at me then retreated as if it knew something about surviving fights, about self-preservation.

"Mr. Baxter?" I asked the old man.

He stopped and turned his head as if someone behind him had spoken that name, then he slapped his free hand against his head as if someone in the back of his own brain had called to him out of his own schizophrenic cacophony. Then he looked back at me.

"You are Samuel Baxter," I reminded. "Your wife was Frances Mary Baxter, and her maiden name was Roberts. Your son is Sheriff Sam Baxter."

"He's the one that brings the food," the old man said.

He pointed the knife at the plastic grocery bag on the bridge. I had dropped the mechanic's rags on top of it and this was a distracting swatch of red in the bottom of my eye.

"Yessir," I said. "I'm sure it's your son, the sheriff, who brings you food. But there's no food in that bag." I pointed at the grocery bag at my feet.

"He said he would bring food tonight. I'm hungry."

"If your son said he would bring you some food tonight I'm sure he will, Sir," I said in as calm a voice as I could manage.

He shifted his eyes toward the twin track behind him, the rutted road that led into the woods in the direction opposite of my place. I had thought I had heard a car on that red clay road in the past and somehow that must have been the way Sheriff Baxter gained backwoods access to his place, to his father, and not attracted attention.

"Do you remember that the man who brings the food is your son, your son who is the sheriff?" I asked.

The old man shrugged and narrowed his eyes at me.

"I know he's the one who wears a badge and handcuffs he puts on me sometimes and that he's the one that took that gun away from him that I got this shirt from but I don't know why he gave *you* that gun."

I tried to parse that out.

"The man with the badge shot the man with the red shirt?"

Old Baxter shook his head.

"Nobody shot him," he told me. "Them that killed the man in the red shirt drowned him." The crazy man jerked his head toward where I had found Buck King the first time in the shallow water near the downed oak tree.

"And then the man with the badge took the gun off the man in the shirt?"

"I had it, found it in the water just down below so it was mine but the man with the badge and handcuffs took that gun I found from me and give it to you so you could kill me with it. He sent you to kill me."

"Why would he do that, Mr. Baxter?" I asked. "Why would your son send me or anyone to kill you?"

"He's tired of me," the old man said. "Tired of taking care of me. That's what he said. That's why he gave the gun to you. The other man he sent couldn't do it and I killed him first with that gun then the one with the badge took the gun away from me so I couldn't protect myself and now he sent you with the gun to kill me so he won't have to take care of me anymore, didn't he?"

"Nossir. The sheriff did not send me here to kill you," I said, tried to sound calm. "Nobody sent me here at all. I just live around here. I come here to the creek all the time. I'm sure you've seen me before here, Mr. Baxter. I walk down here every day almost."

"I have seen you," he said and stared at me as if trying hard to figure out just where he had seen me. "You came to my house to kill me but I killed you with a rock but now you're back, alive just like that drowned one in the red shirt who wouldn't stay drowned—that's why I cut his head off of him."

This was a muddle I was not going to be able to decipher in detail under duress, though I could gather that Old Baxter had seen Tammy Fay and Warnell drowning Buck King, Old Baxter had found Buck's big revolver and, because of his paranoia maybe, shot Joe Pickens Junior with that gun, which the sheriff then found on his father and tried to use to frame me for the death of Joe Pickens Junior, if Sheriff Baxter needed to frame me for something like that, to tie up loose ends or just out of spite.

"I didn't come to kill you, Mr. Baxter."

"That's why I kept the knife," the old man told me. "I took the knife from the man with the red shirt and I kept it because it's my property. I kept the knife. But the one with the badge, he took the gun away from me and gave it to you."

"You did keep the knife," I said, staring at the weapon in his hand.

And I would have thrown the revolver over the railing right then, but for that knife. I should have gotten rid of the gun then anyway, probably. Because a gun is too simple a solution.

But the gun was there.

And I didn't get rid of it. Because I cannot run, am not a good runner, not even fast enough to outdistance a crazy old man.

When he narrowed his eyes at me Old Baxter seemed to be trying to figure me out, understand me, comprehend me. As if he might be the sane one. As if I might be the crazy one.

There was no way, though, that he could know that, if he was or if he wasn't or if I was or if I wasn't.

"He would like to, but he knows he can't kill me," said the old man. "That's why he sent you. That's why the one with the badge sent you to kill me. Because he can't do it himself."

He stated this, but seemed to be asking a question.

I didn't know if this could be true or not. If I had been sent, by the High Sheriff as executioner of this deranged old man, the sheriff's father. Maybe it was all just a coincidence.

I didn't even know if the gun was still loaded with the single cartridge I had put in it, the bullet lifted from Buck King's pocket. I assumed that one cartridge was in the revolver but I hadn't checked.

The gun had been planted under the seat of the Cadillac, by the sheriff I was quite sure. It was evidence against me, just in case such was needed and never meant as a weapon for me, I didn't think.

But there was the one bullet from Buck's pocket, the single shell I had found on the corpse in the creek and loaded into the revolver before I threw that gun into Malcolm's snake pit, a cartridge now likely lodged in some chanced chamber of a rouletted cylinder.

"He sent you," the man repeated. "To kill me for him."

"May be, Mr. Baxter. But I don't think so."

The crazy man moved forward again.

I should have kept talking. Maybe I could have dissuaded Old Man Baxter from the murder in him. I'm a big talker.

But my rhetoric is seldom persuasive.

I should have tried to run.

He was old.

But I was slow.

And there was that stubborn blister still on my left heel.

And I was tired. And sometimes you just get so tired that nothing matters that much and even fear is too much struggle.

And I saw that gleaming huge knife planted between my shoulder blades as I turned tail . . . and

I would not go down that way.

I would, when the time came, face what killed me.

"I killed you once," the old man said. "You remember. You were sneaking around my house waiting to kill me, but I killed you with a rock. I smashed your head in. But then the man with the badge and handcuffs came out here to bring me food and he found you and put hand-cuffs on you and took you off and raised you from the dead."

"You didn't kill me, Mr. Baxter. And no one else has either. Not yet."

The old man began to inch forward raising the knife as he advanced.

"What is dead should stay dead," he said hoarsely.

"You're confused, Mr. Baxter."

I managed to retreat a step, one step.

I put two hands on the gun, fingered the trigger.

"Go back to your house and wait for your son to come, Mr. Baxter," I said in a surprisingly calm voice. "I mean you no harm. You are confused. Just go home now."

He could not hear me. He had not heard any sane thing in a very long time.

He lifted the knife and aimed it at my stomach, pre-tended to twist it in my guts.

I pulled the trigger.

The first chamber was loaded.

The recoil of the revolver knocked me sideways and drove a spike of pain through my wrist.

Samuel Baxter Senior fell dead on his back. Old Baxter was torn apart, like a watermelon had exploded on his chest.

I picked up the mechanic's rag that had swaddled the revolver. I stepped to the dead man and dropped the greasy rag over his face.

Then I turned away, flipped open the cylinder of the gun.

The first chamber had been loaded. The other five had also been loaded.

I drove to UPUMPIT! to make the call.

The dispatcher located the Sheriff at the Crow's Nest.

"Your father is dead," I told Sam Baxter.

The noise of the bar was loud and raucous in the background. The regular world enjoying a regular night. As per usual.

The High Sheriff of Poe County didn't say anything. I could hear him smoking. I could almost hear his brain working. I didn't count the seconds, but it was a while before he spoke.

"You call anybody else?" he asked me.

I remembered what Professor Ford had told me at the Crow's Nest about Sam Baxter, about suiting the lawman's purposes, so I figured my chances were about fifty-fifty with the High Sheriff of Poe County. Maybe even better.

"No," I said. "I can. It was self-defense. But I figured it's your business."

Baxter said nothing more for a long moment.

"I'll take care of it then," he said finally, flatly.

He hung up.

I sat my car in the parking lot of Pick's for a while, past long enough for the sheriff to get there.

At that point there was no point in leaving, running. If Baxter wanted me Baxter would find me. I had placed my bet and shown my own hand and only waited for the house, the High Sheriff, to show his hand.

When he didn't show I went on home, cracked into a quart jar of Smarty Bell's moonshine, established myself on the front porch with my chickens and waited.

❦

I suppose I went to sleep soon after I sat down and only woke up when I felt the rocking explosion that was probably the propane tank or the gas generator or both, blowing up the shed behind the stone house across the creek.

In about a quarter hour I smelled the smoke.

It was the deadest time of morning, around four a.m., the prime time for mischief and madness. I had slept for a long while. If Sheriff Baxter had passed by my place I hadn't noticed.

He could have circumvented County Road 615, taken the expedient backwoods way, as he did usually, I imagined, when tending to his father's rough needs. That back road was not a road I had ever taken, but I guess it was more passable than I had thought—you don't know if you can drive over a bad road until you try to drive over it.

I had never confessed to anything before and it was not liberating, it was just a heavy, moist weight descended on me like a smothering cloud and I just reposed in the chair on the porch for a while, an inert, dead weight myself, just waiting for the sheriff to show up and arrest me or beat me or kill me or thank me.

Whatever way it worked out it would. That die was cast.

There didn't seem much else for me to do than wait, but watch.

After a while I set a ladder against the house and climbed up on the roof and sat there on the rusty tin watching the valley burn. The fire was a lovely, sweat-provoking experience as illicit, dangerous consummations should be.

Not good nor bad so much as moving.

Memorable.

The Wellses came by about six a.m., stood in their pajamas in my front yard, all eight eyes aimed south from whence a dull glow throbbed steady.

My neighbor Jacob didn't seem too worried himself about the fire blazing one point six miles from his house and I don't imagine he had proper homeowner's insurance.

I had more than full coverage on my property and decided that if it burned I would take my new money and move on. If it didn't burn and I could stay, then I probably would stay.

"You think it's going to get to our places?" Jacob asked me as his family moved off, shuffled back home after a few minutes, bored already by this most local and immediate disaster.

"I don't know if it will and don't much care if it does, Jacob," I said.

"That's the way to be about it," he said.

He stood without his family and stared toward the pillar of black smoke feathering into the first fan of dawn.

The valley seemed to pulse with yellow and orange light.

He raised his hand toward me after a spell.

"Guess I'll go on back to the house and rouse the volunteers if I can."

"All right," I said.

CHAPTER 14

The fire raged on until midmorning or thereabouts, then I guess it mostly just quit, burned itself out. Smoke continued to rise against the blushing sky but it seemed the smoldering kind. Ash fell like smudged snow. The danger to my property appeared past.

I climbed off the roof then and fixed myself some breakfast in the anticlimax. I was on the front porch finishing my coffee when the volunteer firemen finally arrived from Doker, parked their antique water pumper in my front yard.

The attendant from the Exxon station, T. Bo, was hanging on the back of the fire truck. Clarence Goodman, the grocery store man, was driving and the watermelon seller, Kendrick, was riding shotgun. The new checkout girl, Shawnda, wearing nothing but a shiny slip, was barefooted and wedged between her boss and the watermelon seller, looking somewhat uncomfortable to be there.

I stepped off the porch and lifted a hand.

"Y'all hungry?" I asked the crew.

"When ain't we hungry 'round here?" T. Bo asked as he swung off the back of the fire truck, then answered his own question. "We always hungry 'round here, Boy. We was born hungry around here."

Altogether they ate two pounds of bacon, a dozen eggs and drank my two weeks' supply of orange juice and a pot and a half of coffee.

I didn't have any milk, nor any bread for toast, but they did not seem to notice these lackings.

They didn't talk much but to grunt. They pointed their forks at what they wanted and when they got what they wanted they nodded cordially at no one in particular. The girl ate and drank the same as the men, though I thought she could have eaten more than that and would have eaten more if the men had not been there or if only I had been there.

Shawnda was pretty in a raw-boned way and tall and shapely, but her teeth were very bad. She held one of her hands near her neck all the time. She watched the volunteer firemen very carefully, but avoided looking at me. The once she did look at me directly, I blushed.

The volunteer firemen seemed in no hurry at all to leave, to go home or go to the fire site. They lingered over their coffee as the announcer on the weather band radio described the fire damage as limited to a few sections of privately held land. The granite ridge of the Grays deflected the fire away from BLM and state park property on the westside and because of the calm weather the flames had never threatened to jump The Little Piney on the southside and get the northside of the creek where Rushing was, where I lived.

There were no reported deaths or injuries, not to man nor to domesticated animals.

"'Bout as good as could be expected," Kendrick suggested.

We all nodded.

"How did y'all get summoned?" I asked as I cleared their plates.

"First off we got a 'nonymous call." Kendrick turned to the pump jockey. "What was it, T. Bo? About three or four a.m.?"

"Little after four a.m. is about right, Kendrick," said the Exxon fellow who picked bacon from his teeth with the corner of a matchbook. "Took us a while however to get dressed and locate one another. Especially our Chief of Auxiliaries, Mr. Goodman here. And then we had to find the fire truck keys. And then about then Jake Wells calls up but it wasn't no water in the pumper to speak of so that was another issue."

The men chuckled at their ineptitude, which seemed exaggerated, both the laughter and the ineptness.

"One thing and another," Mr. Goodman said as he nudged his new grocery store girl, Shawnda, with his shoulder. "Like most the time happens around here, right? We muddled through cloudy waters like we usually do around here, didn't we?"

"Muddy waters," the other two men agreed together.

The girl blushed and tried to cover herself more, but she was not wearing enough slip to cover much. She put a hand around her long bruised neck. She looked at me, her host, first, then at Mr. Goodman, her boss, then at T. Bo, the pump jockey, and then at Kendrick, the watermelon seller and then around again at each of us in turn.

Cᴑ

The firemen reassembled themselves in their gear, trundled out of the house and resituated themselves on their old vehicle, turned around and aimed back at Doker, away from the fire site.

"The Regulars will be out shortly from B'ville," Kendrick said. "Some of those Marshall Island people are still striking over at the Tidy Chicken plant in Danielles and about seven hundred and sixty-nine chickens caught afire or the Regulars they'd have been out here sooner." He shrugged. "But we don't see much danger of your place going up and Mr. Goodman and Shawnda have got to open up the grocery store and T. Bo has got to open up the gas station and I got to get a shower before I go on home to the wife, so we best be off."

"We appreciated your hospitality, Mr. Reynolds," Mr. Goodman said.

He nudged his girl.

Shawnda nodded at me. Shawnda blushed.

"I appreciated yours, gentlemen," I said.

All the volunteer firemen nodded in unison.

"Just lucky it was a calm morning," T. Bo said as he assumed his position on the back of the truck. "Or else the whole hollow could have gone up, droughty as this summer's been. Then we'd a had to do some real work."

His partners laughed very loud.

"It was an unseasonably dry season for a long while," I admitted, of the weather.

"Yes, it was an unusual, awful summer around here this year."

Mr. Goodman, fireman, grocer, bon vivant tooted his horn and drove off.

A few minutes later a pumper from Bertrandville paused in front of the house. A professional fireman warned me to stay away from the fire site until they had declared it safe.

I said I would stay away and I did.

I got a yard broom and started sweeping the ash into neat little piles, but there did not seem to be any real point to that work so I quit it.

———

The sheriff arrived at my place in his Tan-and-White around noon. He was coming from the direction of the creek and he slowed and braked in front of my mailbox.

I stood with the chickens on the front porch, behind the wavy bugscreen, behind the duct-taped Xs.

He sat behind the smoky glass of the cruiser for over a minute.

I counted.

Then his shotgun-side window slid down and he flicked his cigarette onto the straw-dry grass of my front yard.

I stepped off the porch and heeled out the cigarette.

"Mr. Reynolds," he said in a quiet way that invited me to step toward him.

"Sheriff," I said when I was near enough for him to hear me.

Behind the bullet-perforated mailbox I stopped.

I waited for something. I didn't want it, but I expected something from the High Sheriff of Poe County, some-thing revelatory, something terminating. For me there aren't enough tie-ups for all the loose ends in the world and I can live with that. And I am not one who trusts neat solutions or needs them, but everybody else pretty much seems to think that explanations, false and contrived as they may be, are necessary as air.

Loose ends are natural in the world, but most people don't like loose ends.

Still it remains that the best proof that things are how they should be is that they are like they are.

And so, while I didn't want that last word or the next word or any wise word or any more threats from anybody and would have been glad enough to watch Sheriff Bax-ter just drive off without another sound or sign passed be-tween us, I expected it. . . .

Closure.

"The fire burned pretty good," he said. "Once it got started."

I let out a breath I had not realized I'd been holding, as this sounded, as delivered, merely an observation.

"It surely did," I said. "But then it just quit."

"It burned what would burn," the sheriff said. "And then it burned itself out."

He pushed up just a hair the brim of his once-white hat, now smudged gray by smoke and ash, tilted his chin down at me. Then stared ahead through the dirty windscreen.

I waited. He sat his car for a while and didn't smoke a cigarette, didn't move his head, did not blink.

"You understand what it means, Mr. Reynolds, when I say even a crooked stick can hit itself a straight lick in a certain situation?"

"Yes, Sheriff. I understand exactly what that means."

Baxter pulled his hat brim back down, frowned thoughtfully.

"I can fuck you up, Mr. Reynolds. I can fuck up your regular day very bad. Do you understand what I am telling you?"

He didn't look at me when he said this and as this statement and question did not sound a threat I took it as an invitation to parley.

"I can probably mess up your day as well, I think, Sheriff." I said this as true and hoped it was or could be if needed, though I had my doubts.

"You might can," he admitted. "If you live long enough to get to your lawyers." He said this in a mean way, but then he actually smiled at his joke.

I nodded and said, "I guess we're in agreement about the situation."

He put the cruiser back into gear.

"I won't find that revolver, will I, Mr. Reynolds?"

"That gun is history," I said.

His lips curled up. He shook his head slightly, then revved the engine of the Tan-and-White.

"Shame," Baxter said. "That was a good gun."

I was poised to say more, ask a veiled question or two.

But he pressed his finger to his closed mouth, sealed his own lips. Then he pointed that finger at me.

"Word to the wise, Mr. Reynolds," said the Sheriff. "I think you understand me?"

"I think I do," I said and hoped I did.

❧

It was about like that, as I recall it.

I think he said,
As he drove away,
Again,
"Good gun."
But maybe it was,
"Good, son."

❧

That weekend County Road 615 was crowded with sightseers. There's scarce little to do in our neck of the woods and a burned-down forest is a hot ticket. Because it appears a quaint, inviting place from the outside quite a few of the rubberneckers stopped off at First Rushing Evangelical True Bible Prophecy Church of the Rising Star in Jesus Christ on Sunday, so the Right Reverend Mean Joe Pickens Senior allowed his grandson to redo his special music program of singing and harmonica-playing for the assembled in hopes of a good harvest offering of dollar bills and dimes.

I stood in the sideyard of the church, nearby an open

window, and tossed a fifty, folded small, in the collection plate when it came to the end of an aisle and I listened and Malcolm Ray sounded sweet and seemed overjoyed as he sang those old hymns of salvation and played his harmonica. Mean Joe preached a real heartfelt and heated sermon and seemed very pleased with himself as well.

And I didn't feel too bad either, altogether did not feel too bad at all.

We are all sinners, by a natural inclination that is fermented in our daily choice of evil ways, without merit in ourselves, damned and damnable all together from birth to death and every second in between, the Right Reverend reassured.

We are universally corrupt, not one deserving, every one separate and together born in sin and lived in sin and dead in sin from the very moment, the very first second of conception and one of us just as worthless as another of us, and all as worthless of Grace as the others are worthless of Grace as the Word makes plain, which was in the beginning and will be unto The End. Amen.

Still, Grace persists, apparently, rears its fine savior's head here and there, high on the splintered cross of Calvary, elevated above the smoke and fumes of hellsfire that surround us and threaten to consume us, suspended beyond disbelief above this polluted vale of sorry tears and wasted years, above this fouled den of sudden and perpetual iniquity.

But where and when this fine Grace does that, appears to us mortals, I missed in the Right Reverend's message.

I might have been taking a piss in the church outhouse as he was illuminating this particular point.

I know that some believe Grace appears when called upon boldly.

Or anoints us by an informed God's choice.

Or insinuates itself randomly, maybe, like a pleasant virus.

Quite a few of the congregation, uncomfortable with the Right Reverend's reminders of their iniquities, of their intrinsic sinfulness, of their own corruption of mind and flesh and spirit, squirmed all throughout that hellishly fiery preaching, twisted like hooked night crawlers, seated as if slow roasting on smoldering hardwood benches.

Three old front pew women, though, wafted serenely back and forth throughout the extemporaneous sermonizing like loblollies flexing in a stiff breeze, unperturbed by the gale-force edicts directed at their fallen fellows, moved by the message but steady in themselves, settled over their deep, righteous roots. Their giant bosoms cantilevered over enbibled laps, they fanned themselves and steam rose off their capacious, creped backsides like a powderly pungent, like a vaporized holy ghost.

I stood looking in from comfortably outside, in the shade of an elderly pecan tree that leaned over the graceful whitewashed building protectively.

I stood in my sensible walking shoes, with a hat on my bald head and a thermos of beer in my small hands, and did not hardly even break a sweat.

I noticed Miss Ollie there at church, not entirely unfashionably dressed, and I waited outside for her until after the long service was over and then took her for a drive in the Cadillac and we wound up all the way in Hot Springs where we visited the Alligator Farm, the IQ-Zoo and Tiny Town and then removed ourselves to the comfortable Arlington Hotel, right downtown.

It was too early for dancing to the jazz trio but we shared a very nice piece of pie in a downtown diner and then strolled along the upper promenade for a long spell.

"It will be even nicer in the autumn, don't you think, Mr. Reynolds?" Miss Ollie said on the drive back.

I said it would be much the same. But for the foliage.

CHAPTER 15

Malcolm enjoyed his visit to Memphis, even though the momma that abandoned him was nowhere to be found and Elvis was dead.

His own daddy's death seemed to have scarcely fazed the kid.

But then if you don't expect any good from your people then you will never be too disappointed, I suppose. Like Miss Ollie said, a lot of our problems in life are just the results of too high aims combined with too low means, encountering walls too high with ladders too short.

⬥

Tammy Fay's dog Stank wound up staying with the Wellses, since the Wells clan, for all their other numerous faults are, truly, dog people if ever there were and good dogs often prefer not-so-good people, aren't, in fact, very particular at all about who they wind up with as long as they wind up with dog people.

⬥

Mr. Goodman's new checkout girl, Shawnda, moved into the Old Lion, but kept working at Goody's Grocery Store a few hours a week and learned to use the cash register, probably, eventually.

I never heard another word, direct or indirect, from Law Enforcement about what happened on the bridge over The Little Piney.

Sheriff Sam Baxter didn't run for reelection in the fall, but put his family place across The Little Piney up for sale. Burned black and empty as it was now I was not sure who would buy it, but somebody did eventually and turned it into a tree farm for pulpwood pine.

Sheriff Baxter moved to South Texas where he had some connections and got a job with the Drug Enforcement Administration which, I'm sure, suited him well enough.

The grand jury decided that Joe Pickens Junior, the drug dealer who had jumped bail, had been shot and killed by Buck King the bounty hunter who had been trying to apprehend the fugitive from justice, Joe Pickens Junior. During the struggle, Buck King was wounded and drowned. A snapping turtle had decapitated Buck, which outcome seemed suspicious to me, but then snapping turtles can do a lot of damage and they are always hungry for dead flesh.

Warnell Ames would stand trial for the rape and murder of Tammy Fay Smith.

After the grand jury hearings were rather more uneventfully finished than seemed seemly, Dr. Doc Williams retired from his private medical practice in Doker, Arkansas, and moved into a reasonably priced condominium in gulf coastal Mississippi. He learned to play golf I have overheard from Nurse and gave his trial testimony in absentia due to health reasons.

Nurse got a job at Northwest Arkansas Regional Medical Center in Bertrandville, which is where I go weekly for my blood tests and to visit with my new physician who believes in the efficacy of powerful, modern psychotropic medications.

The clinic in Doker became Kountry Kousins Kraft Shoppe.

Once he got going, Warnell Ames confessed to all the summer's murders—the drowning-decapitation of Buck King and the shooting of Joe Pickens Junior—as well as to the rape and murder of Tammy Fay Smith and additionally to the rape and murder of a lady tourist three years before, the rape and murder of Tammy Wynette, the Tate-LaBianca murder mutilations previously attributed to the Charles Manson gang and to the assassinations of Martin Luther King and all the dead Kennedys.

He also confessed to setting fire to about seven hundred and sixty-nine chickens at the Tidy Chicken poultry processing plant in Danielles, though he was nowhere near Danielles when that fire was started.

With the help of a group of anonymously hired, overpaid but excellent criminal defense lawyers imported from Houston, Texas, Warnell successfully pleaded insanity, avoided a potential eventual lethal injection and was incarcerated in a maximum-security mental institution in the Delta region of Arkansas for an indeterminate period of time, most likely life.

Where Miss Ollie visits him irregularly.

I don't believe anyone other than Sam Baxter knows I killed his father.

I haven't told anybody, because I got nobody to tell.

Maybe one day I will have someone to tell about all that.

But I know firsthand that people are devious and hard to trust, so I'm not holding my breath that I will ever have someone I trust enough to share my life and my secrets with.

Since I've none to discuss that killing with, none to really trust it with, I try not to think about it. I don't dwell on what I did because it's not healthy to dwell on things like that.

Naturally the crazy man, Old Baxter, comes to me unbidden in dreams. With the rest of them. My dead.

But truthfully Old Baxter does not seem angry at me. Seems to forgive me as the rest do not, does not linger at my shoulder like the others do, means me no more harm than I meant him.

Sometimes I think I did the old man a favor.

I like to think so.

I know I did his son a favor.

The old man is dead anyway.

And the dead don't need me.

The second day of the New Year next I got an unexpected package.

It had been a Holiday Season less lonely than I was recently accustomed to. I recognized my mother's death date somberly, with a long, slow walk in a stiff new pair of mail-order walking shoes I had gifted myself and then I had a mediocre but filling chipped beef dinner at Miss Ollie's EAT

For Christmas I had a little tree on the front porch that Malcolm helped me decorate with popcorn strings, which the chickens liked. Miss Ollie gave me a modestly priced, but water-resistant Timex wristwatch and I gave her a generous gift certificate to a mail-order leatherwear company since she had pointedly told me that she wanted exactly that.

New Year's Eve I escorted Miss Ollie to Smarty Bell's party at the Crow's Nest.

While I inexpertly steered her that evening around the edges of the small, crowded square of parquet dance floor under the saloon's rotating mirror ball, she confessed that the stress of her husband dying of alcohol poisoning and the stress of living widowed after that for twenty years with her damaged and, apparently, dangerous son Warnell had pretty much ruined her life up to that point in time and, even though she still loved her son and was upset and guilt-ridden about the deaths that past summer and all the other troubles Warnell had caused, she was happy her son had confessed and was gone from her but in a safe place, happy with the way things had worked themselves out, happy that, miraculously, her crooked world had been straightened out a little bit, happier than she had been in a long time, perhaps in forever.

I didn't make any confessions myself to Miss Ollie.

But I did stay fairly sober and did have a pleasant New Year's Eve with her.

And Miss Ollie looked ten years younger after Warnell was locked away, which made her look several years younger than me.

❧

New Year's Day, Malcolm brought the butcher paper–wrapped envelope, out to my place. He thought it might be a belated Christmas present.

There was no return address, no postmark, no stamp. "Mr. Bob Reynolds" was printed in block letters on the front of the envelope.

"PaPaw said it was left outside the store. He told me to bring it on and get his fifty cent for delivery. Is it a present, Bob Reynold?"

I slit the package open with a thumbnail, slid the several photographs out of the envelope and immediately slid them back into the envelope.

"May be, Malcolm Ray," I said. "Or maybe not."

❧

I waited until almost dusk to walk to the creek, stuck the envelope in my heavy parka, locked the chickens on the front porch and turned on their space heater for them so they wouldn't freeze into poultry ice pops.

I walked briskly then because the weather was very cold. After the hottest, driest summer on memorable record the winter had turned cold quick and stayed cloudy.

I had not set foot on the bridge over The Little Piney since that past August, consistently aimed my morning constitutionals in the opposite direction.

The fields were frosty and the livestock illegally in my front forty in them huddled and steaming.

The black forest on the other side of the creek was yet but crystalized stumps, some of them orderly as an orchard.

When I stepped on the iron bridge over The Little Piney my footfalls echoed hollow between the elevated steel and the flat water below it.

The creek was frozen solid along the edges, but in the middle it still ran, fast and green. The downed white oak was a lovely accumulation of icicles. The red-tailed hawk was nowhere to be seen. The fire had seared her aerie and she had moved on.

I extracted the three snapshots from the envelope.

One was the one of Tammy Fay and me having sex in the garden. The one Warnell took, for blackmail if she ever needed it, if she needed to pin the murders on me. I suppose she was just the type that liked to keep all her options open.

The photo was blurry. My eyes were red dots and my bald spot looked like a monk's shaved dome. She looked beautiful. And bored.

One was of her coaxing Doc Williams to an orgiastic climax. An interior shot, maybe in the Old Lion, perhaps even from that year. The doctor's legs were thin and white under his potted belly, marbled by varicose veins. His penis was like a little white bird's egg in a curly nest.

The last was of Miss Ollie in a skimpy mail-ordered leather bra-and-panty outfit.

I ripped two of the pictures into shreds and let those drift out of my hand toward the flowing water. Most of them stuck on the ice, some lightside up and some darkside up.

I folded the third photo in half and tucked it in my parka, zipped the pocket up tight.

I dropped the envelope with my name on it off the bridge and did not watch to see where it landed.

I started the walk home.

The clouded sky was low and dark.

I reached a hand up to pull aside those clouds.

I started to run.

BURN WHAT WILL BURN

Every night I am in the same seared scene, a dream:
Where my dead tell me to burn what will burn,
Starting with them as a paperpoem ream

I choke on every morning-after; the sun's gleam
Stirs the moonshine with sunshine, but then my guts churn.
Toward the night-black same dream:

My dead ignore me as they scull downstream
And pour their gone lives like oil on water from an urn
Themselves. When I call out, first they steam

Then smoke flame, then become flesh, then air. God's scheme
Isn't buttressed by love; it's a test of spurn after spurn
In the same noire dream, sometimes with scream

My dead pull at me from beneath the stream
And I don't fight back, grateful for my turn
To finally join them as dead without, even, a dream.